MW01002192

LOVE AT WILD HARBOR

GRACE WORTHINGTON

Love at Wild Harbor by Grace Worthington

Copyright © 2021 by Grace Worthington

All rights reserved.

Published by Poets & Saints Publishing

ISBN: 978-1-7334110-4-2

Cover Design: Kristen Ingebretson

No part of this book may be reproduced in any form on by an electronic or mechanical means, including information storage and retrieval systems, without permission in writing from the author. The scanning, uploading, and distribution of this book via the Internet or any other means without a legal purchase or without permission from the author is illegal and punishable by law. Please purchase only authorized editions.

This novel is a work of fiction. Names, characters, and incidents are the product of the author's imagination or are used fictitiously. Any resemblance to actual events or persons, living or dead, is entirely coincidental.

Find out more about the author at graceworthington.com

CHAPTER ONE

LILY

Lily Woods stared at her customer, who was biting into a dark chocolate mocha truffle. She had created the new recipe on a whim late last night, and Thelma was the perfect person to try the scrumptious new confection.

"Not bad." Thelma savored the chocolate, pursing her lips. "I like this one." Thelma regularly stopped at Lily's Chocolate Shop to satisfy her sweet tooth and share updates on her latest love interests. "I'm going to need more of these chocolates after what happened with Hank." Thelma stuffed the last of the truffle into her mouth.

"Don't tell me you've broken up with him." Lily refilled the tray of truffles in her display case, trying to figure out how a seventy-six-year-old woman had more juicy gossip to share about her dating life than she did.

"He ate the last of the chocolate. *My* chocolate." Thelma leaned across the counter, frowning like she'd been cheated out of her money. Her face was all wrinkles and lines from years spent on the beach, and she smelled like a bottle of bathroom

1

fragrance spray from the grocery store. "That was the end of Hank. I told him I couldn't see him anymore if he didn't have the manners to ask before he went poking through my cupboards and stealing my chocolate. Next thing you know, he'll be taking my prescription medicine!"

Lily nodded, feigning interest in Thelma's love life, which, from her tone, hadn't gone well lately. Thelma had started dating only five months after her first husband had passed away, certain that Husband Number Two, as she called him, was out there somewhere. That was seven years ago.

On occasion, she would heave a deep-throated sigh and reminisce about Husband Number One, whom she described as "a good man, but a little dull, like a piece of old silverware." Then she would laugh and slap the counter, never one to spend too much time making things rosier than they were.

Thelma had no qualms about sharing the surprising but somewhat uncomfortable details of her love life: namely, who was newly widowed and when she could go out with them. As owner of the local chocolate shop, Lily bore the brunt of Thelma's breakup stories.

"When he left, he looked just like a dog who'd been scolded for eating the steak off my plate. And I haven't heard a word from the man since. Not a single apology! But when he calls, I'm going to tell him that if he wants to be with me, he needs to keep his hands off my chocolate."

Lily offered Thelma a sympathetic smile and wondered how it was possible that Thelma's love life was far more interesting than her own. She hadn't had a date for months, not since she'd broken up with Thomas. Not that she wanted one. She was perfectly happy focusing on her chocolate shop, which took all her time these days. Besides, her luck in the dating department was dwindling now that she had turned thirty. Men always called her "cute" and "sweet," like she was the equivalent of a cream-filled chocolate, just before they dumped her with the ill-fated words, "There's something I need to tell you." She was never seen as wife material, and for the life of her, she couldn't figure out why.

Now, Thelma held her cell phone and scrolled a senior dating app searching for potential candidates since she had broken up with Hank, the chocolate-stealer. She had tried to convince Lily of all the advantages of signing up for a dating app "with men your age, of course."

Lily had kindly resisted. "I'm not going to make a swift judgment about the men I date based on a highly altered photo. Because there's no way anyone uses real photos on those sites."

"This guy looks promising." Thelma turned her phone to Lily, revealing a bald, chubby man with a grim expression, dressed in a flannel shirt, tilting his face like he was trying to read something through his bifocals. He wanted a woman "who takes care of herself and likes long walks on the beach."

"His photo doesn't seem doctored at all. I'll bet he looks just like that!" Thelma said, trying to prove a point.

"I'll say," Lily replied, pretty certain the poor man probably didn't even know how to use a smartphone. It looked like a mug shot.

"I'm just not sure about men in flannel. Is he a lumberjack? It doesn't say in his bio. Oh well, guess I'll find out when I contact him. Maybe Mr. Flannel is the one!" Thelma turned, taking her bag of chocolates, and walked to the door as Lily followed.

"Sorry to keep you so long." Thelma grabbed the door handle and paused to open it. "I thought you might need some encouragement, you know, in the dating department. It's not like you'll be young forever." She leaned toward Lily, her breath smelling like Tic Tacs. "Take it from me, it only gets harder with age."

"Oh, thanks." Lily was pretty sure Thelma and Mr. Chocolate-Stealer had stripped her of any hope of finding a decent date, much less a husband. If anything, they just reinforced her belief that dating apps were a terrible idea.

"I have a feeling you'll be the next one." Thelma waggled a finger at her.

"The next what?"

"The next one who will fall in love, of course."

"Oh, Thelma, I'm sorry to break it to you, but there is *no one* I'm interested in dating, or, for that matter, falling in love with. I'm perfectly happy making chocolates."

Thelma frowned, dissatisfied with her answer. "Well, when you find him, don't say I didn't warn you." Thelma gave a swift nod before stepping outside.

Lily locked the door behind her and headed to the wall she had been painting before Thelma had interrupted at closing time.

She liked making chocolates. In fact, she was beginning to think she could live her whole life making people deliriously happy with her confections and never want for anything more. *Not even a husband.*

Lily dipped her paint roller in the brown paint. The color glistened like the decadent chocolates she made in her shop, shining like brown gems under the pendant lights. A sweet reminder of bliss. A promise of sugary delight.

Across the room, a tray of chocolates waited in a glass case, every one a masterpiece. She had custom-made them for a bridal shower—chocolate hearts with a soft milk chocolate center and a hint of espresso to give a richer flavor. Just looking at them made her want to bite into the soft gooey center. It didn't help that she had forgotten to eat dinner. *Again.*

A soft knock drew her attention back to the present. Her sister Cassidy stood outside waving her toward the door.

"Hang on a sec." Lily put down her paint roller and peeled off her gloves.

As sisters, they couldn't look more different. The oldest girl in the Woods family, Lily ended up the shortest, something both her sisters wouldn't let her live down. Her petite, five-foot-three-inch frame and long, wavy sandy-blonde hair often led strangers to assume she was much younger than her thirty years, a trait her mother said she'd appreciate in time. She wasn't overly beautiful, like Cassidy, or striking, like Megan. Instead, she had been the family tomboy, donning baseball caps and faded Converse sneakers as an awkward tween. Ever the girl next door, with sun-streaked hair and lightly tanned cheeks, she had spent the summers barefoot, smelling of lake water and Coppertone sunblock.

As she grew older, she had come into a quiet beauty, even if her younger sisters' stunning looks overshadowed her own. Lily was scrappy but soft and smelled like a confectioner's shop, all vanilla and cocoa. Men assumed her personality followed suit, expecting to find *sugar and spice and everything nice*, but instead discovered her more nuanced, like a layered dip. Sweet and salty. Tender and tough.

She ran to the door and turned the bolt, letting her auburn-haired sibling into the shop.

Cassidy smelled like jasmine and lilac flowers and wore a lightweight green dress that brought out her eyes, a contrast to Lily's chocolate-smeared apron, covering a paint-stained T-shirt and ripped jeans.

"What are you doing working so late?" Cassidy took off her soft leather bag, stuffed with heavy books, and flung it across a small table.

The shop wasn't huge, but it was the perfect size for a start-up business.

"I'm finally painting the walls. This avocado green has to go. It's hideous. I want this to be a charming café, not an ode to the seventies."

"Lily, I know you want to make this shop look better, but on a Friday night? How are you ever going to meet someone if you spend every night here?"

"Dating someone isn't going to help my shop get off the ground."

"And paint will?" Her sister lifted her eyebrows.

"Okay . . . no. But I'm trying to create a mood here. Chocolate makes everyone feel good." She dipped her roller in the paint and spread it across the wall.

"There won't be any chocolate shop if you work yourself to death. You need to take a break. Get a life outside this business."

"And do what? Sit around waiting for Mr. Right to come knocking? Because I've done that, and all I got were crickets." Lily slid her paint roller across the hideous green. "What do you think? Does it work?"

Cassidy stood back, admiring her work. "It's fabulous. Like the wall is made of chocolate."

"That's exactly what I wanted you to think."

Cassidy walked to the glass case and eyed the hearts. "Speaking of chocolate, these look amazing. Who knew the former banker turned chocolatier was so talented?"

Lily stopped painting and pushed a stray wisp of hair out of her eyes, remembering her former life as a desperately unhappy loan officer at the local bank. The job had sucked the life out of her soul until the day she had stood at her desk and announced she was quitting—the most freeing thing she had ever done. "Don't even think about stealing one. They're for a wedding shower."

"Who's the lucky bride?"

"Jessica Bradford."

"I heard she met her fiancé at last year's summer beach festival. Which goes to show you, if you're stuck working all the time—"

"I don't want to hear it."

". . . you'll never meet Mr. Right," Cassidy finished.

"I'm not interested right now. Not after what happened with—"

"I know. Thomas didn't deserve you."

"That's putting it mildly. More like a world-class jerk. For once, I'm finally doing something to turn my life around, move forward, just like Dad taught us. By the way, did you stop and see him today?"

Cassidy sat down at a table. "Yes, before I came over. His physical therapy appointment didn't go well. Never mind that he's stubborn as a mule. Ever since his stroke, everything has been hard for him. Relearning to walk again is going to be a battle, but if we all cheer him on, who knows what he can do?"

Cassidy had always been Daddy's baby girl, and Lily appreciated her younger sister's tender, emotional heart. As Lily and her siblings grew up, they hadn't always gotten along, but now that they were adults, Dad's stroke was bringing them closer together.

"I've been sneaking him extra chocolates after work. It's the only thing that cheers him up."

"I know your famous chocolate therapy all too well. But I am never going to fit into my jeans if I keep eating yours."

"Cass, you don't look like you've ever gained a pound. Really, I can't believe some guy hasn't swept you off your feet yet."

Cassidy rested her elbows on the table, leaning her chin on her hands. "I'm not sure working in a bookshop is a great place to meet eligible bachelors. But at least I get out, unlike *someone* I know . . ."

"I'm perfectly content *not* getting out and have resigned myself to embracing the glorious title of spinster and owning a bunch of cats." She was trying to view her situation objectively, to accept a life of singleness, like a detached observer. So far, it wasn't working.

"Really, Lily, I can't ever imagine you as a spinster."

"If my recent bad luck with men is any indication, then I'm

destined to it. At least, I'll know how to make delicious chocolates. There's only one problem. I need to finish this painting tonight because I have a big chocolate order for later this week."

Lily spread more paint across the wall. She was on a deadline.

No time for love. That's what she told herself.

It was so much easier than believing in a fairy tale.

CHAPTER TWO

LILY

L ily stepped back to examine her work. One wall done. At this rate, she'd never finish tonight.

"Do you have an extra paint roller? I'll pitch in." Cassidy stood. "I could see if Megan and Matt are available to help." She grabbed her phone to text their siblings.

"Tell them I owe them my firstborn in return for their labor." Lily assessed the newly painted wall. Dad would be proud. Only a few months earlier, he had suffered a massive stroke that had left him hospitalized. Now that he was home, he couldn't walk without help. Even though the doctors had told her mom he was lucky to be alive, Lily wondered whether surviving a stroke only to be a prisoner in your own body, was really *lucky*.

She didn't understand why this had happened to her dad, one of the most selfless people she knew. Now, he sat helpless in a wheelchair, learning to do basic things again, grappling with the fact that he might not ever make a full recovery. Even more concerning was that he was at risk of having another stroke, something that weighed heavily on the whole family, but especially Lily, since she was the worrier in the family.

Another knock interrupted Lily's thoughts. Meg, her dark-haired sister, stood outside waving. As she entered, she brought in a burst of warm air. "I just got off work and saw your text. Late night party?"

"More like pitch in to help your sister." Cassidy handed Megan a roller. "Matt's on his way."

"I can wield a paintbrush like a pro." Meg imitated some ninja moves while Cassidy shook her head.

"Meg, are you sure?" Lily placed another drop cloth on the floor. "You've got to be exhausted after working all day."

"I've been sitting at a desk for too long. Besides, I needed a break from another pet rescue story." Although Megan loved her job at the *Wild Harbor News*, she often worked long hours, writing articles that were, according to her, no more than fodder for town gossip. It wasn't her dream job, but it gave her the experience to move up to a big news outlet.

"I can't tell you how much this means to me for both of you to pitch in like this," Lily said.

"You're not going to cry, are you?" Megan punctuated the air with her roller. "Because you look like it."

"They're called allergies, and I can't help it if my eyes water." Admittedly, she always had cried too easily, despite her tough exterior. The embarrassing trait had earned her the label, "too sensitive." Wasn't that what her ex, Thomas, had told her?

"Don't be a baby," he'd say when she turned the slightest bit teary, cocking his head and giving her a patronizing smile, as if she were a little girl who needed to be reminded how to act in public.

In response, she'd closed off her emotions like turning off the water hose. *Sealed and shut.* At the time, she hadn't realized this was only the beginning of his control issues. She turned back to open another paint can.

Matt walked in the door next, his sleek dark-brown hair tousled by the wind off the lake. As the oldest sibling and a firefighter, he had a commanding presence that softened whenever he smiled. Dressed in joggers and a T-shirt, he was the weekend adventure hunter who competed in triathlons and swam laps in the lake *for fun* when he wasn't fighting fires.

"You guys will never believe what I heard today," Matt said as he scrolled his phone.

"How about first saying hello to your favorite sister?" Megan held out her arms.

"Okay." Matt turned to Lily and gave her a side hug. "Hello, sis."

Cassidy smacked him on the arm playfully, while Megan held the roller to his face. "You're lucky I don't roll this right over your smirk."

"Whoa." Matt held up his arms in surrender. "Okay, you're all my favorites. Well, most of the time."

Megan made a face.

Matt sat on a nearby table. "I heard some big news when I was at Brewster's for lunch with the mayor for a firefighter appreciation event."

"What's the news?" Megan dipped her roller back in the tray. "You always give us the dirt before we hear about it at the paper. Maybe I can get the scoop before my boss."

Megan was chomping at the bit to write more front-page stories, even if only in the local paper. So far, her boss had assigned her pieces buried deep in the paper's second section, covering ladies' social luncheons and student of the month at the local school.

Matt set his phone on the table, a smile playing across his lips. "You guys ever hear of *The Property Bachelor*?"

"You mean Alex Briggs' TV show?" Cassidy poured more paint into her tray. "He's only the biggest name on the Home Improvement Network right now."

Lily's stomach did a flip at the sound of Alex's name, her childhood friend turned high school crush. She was sure Alex wouldn't give her the time of day now that he had made it to the big leagues, but hearing his name flooded her with a hit of dopamine. Ever since he had chosen Priscilla Todd as his date to the senior prom, Lily had held a grudge against Alex.

"Alex Briggs is coming to town to do an episode of his home improvement show," Matt said. "The mayor just got word on Friday. He didn't want to say anything until they had secured the site and received approval to move ahead with the project."

Lily's sisters looked at her. It was no secret that she had fallen hard for the handsome high school jock turned TV star. But that seemed a lifetime ago, long before she knew what heartbreak was. When he'd left Wild Harbor, she had promised to forget all about Alex for good. And she had. Until *now*.

Megan put her roller down. "You're kidding me. Wild Harbor is going to be on Alex's home improvement show? My boss is going to be floored. I thought Alex would never come back here."

"I'm sure everyone is going to be flocking to see him." Lily knelt and placed her roller in the tray. "Not that I'll be one of them." She picked up a brush and started edging the corner.

"Come on," Cassidy said. "You don't want to at least see how your high school crush looks now?"

"I've seen the commercials, but I don't watch the show." Lily focused her attention on the corner. "And he's *not* my crush." Part of her wondered what he was like now that he'd made it big in Los Angeles, while the other part resented his homecoming. Now, *of all times,* when her luck was in the toilet.

"He's the perfect blend of nice-guy-next-door meets handsome hunk," Megan added. "Ideal for the show. No wonder he's a hit."

A hit. *Of course.* Everything about Alex had screamed success in high school, causing her to fall hard for him. *Embarrassingly* hard. Growing up, he had been the only kid on the street who liked to play basketball, forging a friendship with her grounded in competition. As they grew into awkward adolescents, he had sat on her porch swing, practicing his guitar and making up cheesy songs about teenage angst. Alex had wanted to be an actor back then but also had picked up some impressive construction skills from his father. He had merged the two talents, auditioning for the show a few years ago.

Now that he was the darling of the home improvement world, he never came back to Wild Harbor. A fact that suited Lily just fine.

It seemed everything in her life had gone awry, while Alex had hit gold. If he was returning to town, she had to avoid crossing his path. She couldn't bear his pity.

"Lily? Hello. Earth to Lily. Did you hear me ask for the paint?" Matt nodded toward the can by her feet.

"Oh, sorry. I was thinking." Lily put down her paintbrush and handed Matt the can as he grabbed a brush.

"Is it Alex? I can tell the news rattled you, like you just saw a ghost. I thought maybe it'd be fun to get the gang back together . . ." Matt dipped his paintbrush and covered the high spots Lily couldn't reach.

"No." Her answer slipped out before she could stop it. "I'm not interested in seeing Alex. You can get the guys together if you want, but I have too much on my plate. The shop. My grand opening coming up. I don't need to listen to Alex brag about his accomplishments. I'm sure his grand Los Angeles lifestyle is a far cry from how he grew up as a contractor's son in a small town."

"How do you know he's changed?" Cassidy stepped on a chair and continued painting.

Lily stopped and faced her siblings. "Because everyone changes, including me. I'm no longer the stupid girl with a crush, right?"

"Okay, fair." Cassidy flopped onto a chair nearby, her curls cascading across her shoulders. "But what if Alex wants to see you? You were always close. I swear he had feelings for you in high school."

"I don't think so. Why else would've he asked Priscilla to the prom?"

"Because he was scared to ask you. Afraid of rejection. It's the age-old male ego problem," Megan said, as if she were a psychiatrist diagnosing a patient.

"Hey," Matt interrupted. "Watch what you say about our egos."

"I'm just stating the facts," Megan said.

"What if he wants to get together?" Cassidy stepped down from her chair.

"Tell him I'm busy." Lily turned back to her partially trimmed wall. "If there's one thing I know, it's that I don't want to see Alex again."

She'd make sure of it. The last thing she wanted him to know was how tough life had been.

Before Lily could go on, her phone buzzed on the table nearby. "It's Mom." She picked up the phone, worry bubbling up inside. "What's up?" She listened a minute and frowned. "Oh, no. I'll be right there."

Lily ended the call. "Dad's fallen. Again. I'm going to check on him." She rushed to grab her purse and surveyed the mess.

"I'm coming too," Matt said. "You can't lift him by yourself."

Cassidy put down her roller. "Don't worry about the paint or coming back to close. Megan and I will take care of things, then we'll be right there."

Lily's face melted into a weary smile as she grabbed her keys. "You guys are the best." Then she turned to Matt. "Meet you there in a few minutes?"

He nodded as she ran out the door toward her car a few blocks away. Alarm bells in her head pushed her forward. *I hope it isn't another stroke.* Why was she always thinking of the worst every time something happened to her dad? She already knew the answer: when tragedy strikes, you can't help but worry about when the other shoe will drop.

Lost in her thoughts, Lily absentmindedly bolted across the intersection. A pickup slammed on its brakes, screeching to a stop only inches from her body, leaving the smell of hot rubber in the air. Lily escaped the near miss by sprinting to the other side, barely registering how close she'd come to catastrophe.

The truck honked. A muffled voice yelled something.

Lily didn't have time to look back. She silently prayed, *Please let Dad be okay, and don't let it be another stroke.*

She reached her car, jumped into the driver's seat, and squealed onto the street, accelerating toward her childhood home. She only had one thing on her mind—her father. She only hoped she could reach him in time.

CHAPTER THREE

ALEX

It wasn't the homecoming he had planned. Alex had imagined arriving in town during the day, when the town was filled with slow traffic and children were jumping sprinklers after school. He knew his first stop: Brewster's, where he'd get at least a dozen hugs from the older ladies. Then he'd sit on a barstool, lingering over old memories, helping himself to Ada's hot apple pie dripping with gooey, cinnamon-laden filling.

Home. *Finally.*

But life rarely worked out as planned. He had learned that early in life.

His flight had been delayed, causing him to arrive in Wild Harbor soon after the town had shut down for the night, like a ghost town in a Wild West movie. He was headed down Main Street, peering at the darkened shop windows, when a woman sprinted into the intersection, oblivious to everything but where she was going.

What in the world?

His heart skipped a beat, the same way it did when a doe jumped into the road in front of his car. Not until the glow of his headlights caught her flowing hair did Alex realize he knew this woman. His breath caught in his throat as he slammed on his brakes.

Is that—Lily?

A rush of adrenaline pulsated through his body as the bumper of his car stopped inches from her. Even though it had been almost eight years since he had last seen her, he would know her profile anywhere.

Lily Woods.

She hadn't changed one bit. Still the petite blonde with the stubborn look who could stop traffic. *Maybe even his heart.*

He put his window down. "Hey, Lily!" But his engine drowned out his voice as she raced across the street. He watched her disappear, then heard a car starting in the distance. The screech of tires echoed in the silent town. He could follow and find out where she was running. But the dull ache of regret told him to back off.

She's not yours anymore, remember?

Still braked in the street, he studied the storefronts, which appeared exactly the same as when he left. The old hardware store where his dad stopped for supplies. The ice cream shop that only opened during summer, known for their wildly famous Wild Harbor Sundae—a decadent banana split loaded with chocolate, caramel, and whipped cream. The street that led to his favorite spot, the park that overlooked the beach, where he had sat on summer nights with Lily and dreamed about his future.

His phone rang, snapping him back into the present and stealing Lily's memory as quickly as she had appeared. It was Cameron, his buddy from grade school, who was one of the few he had kept in touch with since he'd left.

"Hey, man, where are you?" Cam's voice was barely distinguishable above the crowded restaurant noise.

"Main Street. Just wandering through town, checking out the old haunts."

"Reliving your youth, huh? There will be time for that. Still want to meet at Brewster's?"

"I thought they closed at nine?"

"Yeah, until your secret arrival leaked. They kept the place open so you can eat dinner. What do you want from the grill? I'll order carryout to deliver to your rental."

"I've been craving a Brewster's burger ever since I left town. Throw in a large fry and slice of apple pie. I'm hungry."

"You've got it. Should I invite some friends tonight? In case you didn't know, the guys have still been meeting all these years. Our group is pretty tight."

Alex felt a twinge in his stomach, realizing his four friends from high school were still meeting without him. "Oh, man. I'm pretty tired, and I start the job tomorrow at six. I want to see the old gang but not tonight."

"Who are you calling old?" Cam teased. "Okay, see you soon."

Alex hung up and thought about the club he had formed with these four guys at sixteen. They had all been lifeguards and their friendship had been cemented through long summer days at the shore. They'd called themselves "The Brothers" because they were more like family than friends, and it seemed cool to give the group a name. Of the five guys, he was the one who had abandoned them to chase his dreams. Now, they were welcoming him back as if he had never left.

He turned on a side street to find his bearings and noticed the lights of a small shop spilling onto the sidewalk. He slowly pulled up and recognized the familiar faces of his childhood neighbors. Curious to find out where Lily was going, he parked his truck and took a deep breath. Running his fingers through his dark hair, he walked to the door and slowly knocked on the glass.

Megan turned around, her eyes widening in surprise. "Well, if it isn't the star of Wild Harbor!" She threw the door open and pulled him in by the sleeve of his denim jacket, just like high school all over again. "I haven't seen you in ages, Alex. How are you?"

"Freezing, actually."

"Did you forget how temperamental lake weather is in May?"

"I live in California. We don't need warm clothes."

"Welcome to Michigan." Megan spread her arms wide. "Where it doesn't get warm until June . . . in case you forgot."

Cassidy walked up to Alex with a warm smile. "Hey, Alex," She gave him a hug and stepped back. "We're just glad you're home. Don't worry, it's supposed to be seventies and sunny the rest of the week."

Home. The words still sounded strange.

"We heard the news," Megan interrupted. "The episode you're doing here. You'll draw quite the crowd. So, where's the house?"

"Can't say yet. It's a secret."

Cassidy shook her head. "You've got to be kidding. We are the people who knew you before you were famous. Don't we get some special privileges?"

"I'd love to tell, but the show doesn't allow me to. I haven't even seen the place yet, but it's a beachfront home. It's surprising that any of the homes on the water need repaired."

"Then you haven't seen Lily's fixer-upper." Megan wiped paint off the back of her hand. "She bought this wreck of a home on the beach six months ago with dreams of repairing it."

"Herself?"

"Sort of. With Dad's help. That was before she quit her plush bank job." Cassidy folded a drop cloth. "Now she has her hands full trying to make this shop a success."

"Lily owns this place?" He walked to the display case with truffles lined up in trays, their glossy chocolate exteriors glistening under the lights. "I didn't know she was interested in chocolate. How's the business going?" He regretted not telling Lily he was coming into town, but something had held him back. A promise made to himself long ago.

The girls paused and gave each other a look. "Life has not exactly been easy for our parents." Cassidy poured her extra paint into the can. "Did you hear about our dad?"

Alex turned around. "No, what happened?" He remembered Lily's father as the guy who always was willing to help, no matter what. When Alex had a fender bender in high school, it was Bill Woods who had shown up and helped him fix it.

"He had a stroke three months ago and still hasn't fully recovered." Cassidy's paint slowly dripped off the tray into the can. "Lily bought the chocolate shop just a month before, but it's been hard to get off the ground during Dad's recovery. She feels like she has to pull her weight in the family. No one puts that pressure on her, but she insists."

"Plus, she bought a house that's falling down around her, thinking she'd have time to fix it up," Megan said. "It was bad timing. There's no way she has time, on top of everything else."

"Man, that's rough." Alex felt a pang of guilt that he had avoided keeping in touch. "Does she have anyone to help?"

"You know Lily." Megan gathered the paint supplies. "She's doesn't ask for help because she feels like a bother. Would rather work herself to death first. She was painting alone until Cass and I showed up. Then Mom called and said Dad fell, and she rushed home to help while we cleaned up."

So, that's why she was flying through town. Alex sized up the painting supplies. "How about I take care of this, so you can check on your dad? That is, if you trust me. I can knock out this project tonight."

"Tonight?" Megan's mouth fell open. "Aren't you tired?"

"Painting is something I enjoy. It's soothing, actually."

Cassidy shook her head. "Alex, you don't have to do—"

"I want to. Just promise me one thing. Don't tell Lily. You know how she gets."

"You mean her stubborn streak?" Megan laughed. "I'm surprised you haven't forgotten."

He smiled. "Some things don't change." He grabbed a tray of paint and remembered how Lily had held a grudge after some disastrous final weeks of their senior year. Even though he had apologized, she wouldn't let him live it down. *Probably still won't.*

"Now pass me a paint roller."

"You actually do this home renovation stuff?" Megan waved her hand toward the painted wall.

"How do you think I paid rent in Hollywood before I landed this gig? I took on odd jobs between acting roles. Always did like painting the best. There's something about covering up an old wall that's invigorating. Paint can change a whole room." He swept the roller across the wall while Megan poured more paint into the tray.

Cassidy put on her jacket. "Have you talked to Lily since you left?"

"Uh, no. I saw her briefly after my dad's funeral, before I left for Hollywood eight years ago. But she was still mad about the way I'd left things our senior year of high school. Probably still is."

A look passed between Megan and Cassidy. "Oh, we know what happened." Cassidy walked to the sink. "First, the prom incident with Priscilla, then the porch swing disaster. Lily was— how shall we put it?—a bit miffed. She seemed to think—"

". . . I was a jerk?" He filled in the words, trying to forget how he had interfered with her prom date then driven her away for good after a failed attempt at kissing her on the porch swing a week later. "I regret how I ended our senior year. *Big time.* I wouldn't be surprised if she avoids me while I'm here."

"She's planned on it." Megan crossed her arms. "Especially when she finds out you helped paint her shop."

"Which she will not. *Ever.*" He gave Megan and Cassidy his sternest expression. "Seriously. I don't want her to know."

Cassidy scrubbed the paint off her hands. "She might talk to you if she knew."

"I don't want her to think I'm doing this because of some ulterior motive."

As he swept the roller across the wall, he wondered *exactly* why he was here again. He had promised himself he wouldn't get involved in her life while he was home, but his curiosity was too strong. "So, has Lily settled down?"

"Quite the opposite. She's sworn off dating for good. Especially after—" Megan caught herself mid-sentence after her sister mouthed the word *no.*

He stopped painting. "After what?"

"Listen, I shouldn't divulge details about Lily's love life. Wouldn't be fair. You can ask her yourself."

Like she'd tell me. "I'm the last person Lily wants to talk to." He smiled, shrugging it off as a joke. "But if you guys would be up for it, I'd love to catch up sometime."

"Sure, let's plan for it. Pizza at George's?" Megan turned to her sister, who was dragging her out of the shop. "I hate to leave you with this mess, but—"

"No, please go." He gave them a wave as they left.

Maybe if he earned Lily's trust, she might open up. But that would take putting himself out there. Something he couldn't take a chance on. After what had happened in his past, he'd never let himself take that risk again.

CHAPTER FOUR

LILY

L ily woke to the rumble of a truck engine next door
followed by voices outside her window. Her quiet beach
cottage rarely had any noise other than the sound of a neighbor's car ambling down the street. Tucked into a quiet residen-
tial neighborhood, the sleepy stretch of beach houses rarely saw
any action.

Scrambling out of bed, she discreetly peered out the window
toward the street, trying to hide her silky pajama set. Several
large trucks were parked outside, with one blocking her small
drive. A group of men stood in the yard next to hers.

Did someone buy the empty house next door?

The dilapidated cottage had sat empty for a year. The
owners refused to drop the inflated price because they knew the
high value of beach property in the area. But given that the
dwelling needed a total overhaul, she wondered who had finally
caved. The cottage, with its peeling blue paint and a porch
nearly falling off, needed some major TLC. The entire home
needed gutting, and most people saw it as too much work to be

worth the effort. Although the place was an eyesore, Lily's home ran a close second.

She looked around at all the repairs she still hadn't touched. The peeling paint. The closet door that would no longer close. The leaky bathroom faucet. The sagging porch. The window that was cracked. The roof that needed new shingles.

She sighed and walked to the kitchen to make her morning coffee. She would finish the repairs, even if it took a lifetime. She filled her coffee carafe in the sink and looked at the dated 1920s-style cabinets that desperately needed a new coat of paint.

She had bought this house, despite its flaws, when she worked at the local bank in a posh salaried position. She had been unhappy with her job processing loan applications, but was saving for her dream home on the lake. Most of the beach houses weren't even close to her price range, until this eyesore came on the market, with a *For Sale By Owner* sign in the front yard.

Lily had known this was the one. She'd made a beeline to meet the owner, an older widower who was moving into a retirement home. She'd stopped by with her homemade fudge and a desperate offer, thinking she'd never convince him.

When he'd taken one bite of her fudge, he'd said, "You can have the house for a reasonable price. Just keep making this fudge."

And she had. That was when Lily's Chocolate Shop was born.

In less than six months, she bought a falling down beach bungalow, quit her bank job, and opened a chocolate shop after completing a chocolatier training intensive. Her friends thought she was crazy. She called it her midlife crisis at thirty.

In the future, when her shop was making money, she would turn this place into her dream home. A place where she could fall in love. Wake up to a thousand sunrises next to her husband. Chase seagulls on the beach with her kids.

Even though she remained painfully single, she knew these dreams like every chocolate recipe she had ever made. But for now, she had to focus on making money and taking care of her dad.

Last night, he had tried to get out of bed and had fallen, but by the time she'd arrived, he'd acted like it was nothing. She had been relieved it wasn't another stroke, but she was still worried that his balance wasn't improving, especially since their house contained a steep staircase. "Just a bump on the head," he'd told her. "I'll be fine."

When she'd left, Dad had been sleeping peacefully, even though Mom had still seemed shaken. "I'm concerned this is our new normal. What happens when I'm not here and he falls?"

Lily had hugged her mom and whispered, "You know how stubborn Dad is. He won't rest until he can walk again. And his speech has already returned to normal."

She'd kissed her mom on the cheek before heading home.

Dad's fall last night had sparked an idea. Something preposterous, in fact. *What if her parents moved in with her?*

She was single, and they had always dreamed of living on the beach. It seemed like the perfect solution, *except* that her house was not even close to being done. She needed some major remodeling work, and there was no way Lily could afford it after buying this house.

Her mind spun with ideas as the coffee brewed, filling her home with the warm aroma. *There had to be a way.*

Lily threw on an old T-shirt and worn jeans while she sipped her coffee. She figured nobody would see her today while she painted her chocolate shop except Ralph the mailman, who was always too busy to care how she looked. *Thankfully.*

She threw her hair into a messy bun, decided to forgo

makeup, and grabbed her purse. Lily walked outside, where the truck still blocked her drive. She crossed her arms and sighed. *If they had actually looked to see where my drive was—*
She cleared her throat to get their attention.

Nobody responded.

Well, then. I'll show them who's in charge around here.

She readied herself for battle as she crossed the yard to explain that they could not, under *any* circumstances, set up shop in her drive. With a tumbler of coffee in hand, she beelined toward a pair of men. One pointed at the outside of the house while the other took notes on his phone.

"We're going to have rebuild it from scratch," one said. "The wood is totally rotted out. If we tear it down and start over—"

Lily narrowed her gaze and cleared her throat. "Excuse me, I was just wondering who blocked my driveway, because the vehicle needs to be moved. *Now.*"

The men turned around.

Lily's stomach dropped as she looked at the extraordinarily handsome man with the brilliant blue eyes and broad shoulders.

Alex.

She'd know him anywhere. Although he was older, time had only enhanced his features. With a day-old scruff covering his chiseled jaw and his dark tousled hair, he filled out his shirt better than he ever had in high school. He smelled like leather and musk, and looked like he bathed in mountain streams while hiking the Pacific Crest Trail.

"Lily? What are you doing here?" Two lines appeared between his eyebrows as he studied her.

"I live here. Well, not *here*, but next door." She gestured with her hands, waving vaguely toward her porch. "I was wondering the same thing. What are you doing here?"

Alex looked at the other guy, and a silent message passed between them. "I'm under contract not to say."

"Oh. Wait." She pointed to the cottage. "Is *this* the place you're going to renovate for your TV show?"

Alex only smiled and shrugged. "Like I said, I can't say. Top secret."

Lily's mouth fell open, and she shook her head. "No way. That home has been empty for a year. Nobody has bought it because it's an overpriced disaster. Why would you want to tackle that?"

"Lily, have you seen my show? We take the worst properties and fix them up until they're ready to sell."

"Sell? In other words, it's about the money?" She crossed her arms and narrowed her gaze at him. Never mind that the house was a complete eyesore and wasn't helping her property value.

"Not for me. But if I lost money on a house, I wouldn't have a job anymore."

"Please don't tell me you're going to tear it up."

"You mean with the moldy walls? The rotted wood?" He gave her a teasing smile that was seriously cute. Even dressed in a T-shirt, she could tell he was strong. He looked like he could chop down trees and build his own log cabin singlehandedly.

She felt the heat rising in her cheeks as she looked away. "Uh, no. I mean the wood floors and molded trim. All the stuff that makes these historic cottages unique."

"I try to keep as much as I can. But it'll depend on the water damage inside. So, which house is yours?" Alex glanced past her cottage at the nicer houses on the block.

"Uh, mine is this one." She pointed over her shoulder and cringed inwardly. "The other house that's falling down in the neighborhood." She smiled and tried to pass it off as a joke, but could feel her face deepen to red.

"A fixer-upper, huh? I know some people who could help with that."

"I'm doing it with my father's help." Lily looked away, knowing Dad was in no shape to work on her home.

"I'd love to see it sometime. I could give you some advice—"

"No, no," she answered quickly. "I already know what it's going to look like. Gray walls. Quartz kitchen counters. New tile in the bathrooms. It's going to be charming someday."

"I'm sure it will be." Alex nodded, amused by her description. Her heart fluttered as she met his gaze. Her mind floated back to the evenings they'd spent on the porch swing, listening to Alex strum his guitar softly while lightning bugs flashed like tiny stars in the darkness.

She tilted her head toward the huge truck blocking her narrow drive. "Listen, I'd love to chat, but I need to get to work, and you're blocking my way."

"Yeah. Let me get the boys on it." He flagged one of the men unloading equipment. "Hey, Chad, can you move the truck?" Then he turned back to Lily. "So, I'd love to catch up sometime. Maybe see your family?"

She shifted uncomfortably, glancing toward the beach. Sailboats dotted the distant horizon. She was good at hiding her feelings, but looking into his eyes made her feel like a foolish young girl. Spending time with him would be the worst thing she could do after her ugly breakup with Thomas, which had left her wary of ever trusting another man.

She looked back at his blue eyes, the same ones she remembered so well from high school. She had wanted nothing more than for him to only have eyes for her, but after he'd danced with Priscilla at prom, his eyes gazing into hers, her heart burned with fury.

"I'm really busy. So, we'll see." She didn't want to say no, but it was for the best. For *her* best.

His face fell. "No problem. If something opens up, let me know."

He probably wasn't used to women turning him down once he had achieved rock-star status. But Lily wasn't *any* woman.

"Sorry." She lifted her chin and stepped away. It was bad

enough he was making her heart pound faster. She pushed the feeling down. No man would make her feel weak again.

She gave Alex a quick wave and walked to her car. Watching him work on the house next door was going to be hard.

As she drove to the shop, her mind was engrossed in one problem: how to stay out of Alex Briggs' way. Could she work long hours and brush him off completely?

Maybe. But she had to be resolute. Avoid him at all costs.

No matter what my heart says.

She walked inside and stopped suddenly, floored.

Her shop was completely painted.

CHAPTER FIVE

ALEX

"Are you sure we can't change to a different house?" Alex asked Phil, the show's producer, on the phone.

He had spent the entire day trying to make plans for the renovation, and it was becoming clear it would be a monster project. Besides the house being an absolute nightmare, Lily obviously didn't want to see him.

A change of venue would solve everything.

"No, the deal's done," Phil replied. "We bought the property. You're going to have to move forward, even with all that water damage. Gut the whole thing. If we take a loss, that's fine. But it's settled. Oh, and the chick next door? You can deal with her, right? It's only a month."

"Sure."

How was he going to get through a month?

Alex was certain Phil probably had his feet propped on his posh office desk back in LA, drinking his fourth cup of coffee of the day. He didn't want to hear Alex's problems. Never mind that Alex was making him loads of cash.

"Not even the slightest chance we could sell it to another investor?"

"Nope. No chance. Sorry, man. Hey, they got a little beach there?"

"Little? It's Lake Michigan." Somehow, Californians thought their beach was the only one that counted.

"I'm sure there are some pretty ladies. Go have fun."

Alex rolled his eyes. "Whatever. Thanks, Phil." His boss seemed to forget—or intentionally ignore—that Alex had grown up in the church and believed that if he ever found *the one*, he'd be faithful to his marriage vows. He wasn't looking for a weekend fling. Besides, how could he have fun when this huge project loomed?

He needed to map out every last detail until all the puzzle pieces fit. The last thing he needed was a woman to complicate things.

He looked at his watch: 7:36 p.m. He'd worked right through dinner, and his stomach was rumbling. He quickly sent a group text to Matt, Megan, and Cassidy.

Alex: Anyone up for pizza tonight? It's on me.

Cassidy: Yes. Can't wait!

Matt: Can I bring Cameron?

Alex: Sure.

Megan: You're asking Lily too, right? She'll feel left out if you don't.

Alex: She won't say yes.

Megan: She told me where your house project is. Right next door.

Alex: Just for the record, she doesn't want to see me.

Megan: If you don't ask her, I will. And I'll tell her who finished the paint job!

If Alex hated anything, it was blackmail. Now, he had no

choice. He walked to her home and knocked on the door.

"Alex?" Lily stood in the doorway, chocolate smeared across her apron. "I didn't know you were still there. I figured you were done for the night."

"I'm usually the last to leave. Long day of figuring out details. You were right, by the way. The house is in horrendous shape." He paused, suddenly feeling like a tongue-tied teenager.

It's not like I'm asking her out.

"Do you want to come in?" She swung the door open wider, the light from inside cascading across her porch.

This was a mistake. He shouldn't ask her to dinner. "You're not still mad we blocked your drive?"

"No, but I will be if you do it again." She gave him a playful smile that had an edge to it.

"Okay, okay. I'll make sure the guys are careful." He lifted his hands in surrender. "Or you can take it out on me."

"Sounds like a deal. I'm sorry if I came across a little . . ." She searched for the word.

"Mad? Irate? Irritated?" A sly grin appeared on his face.

She hit him gently on the arm. "No. I was going to say strong. As a woman, I sometimes have to say things a certain way to get taken seriously."

"Really? It shouldn't be that way."

He stepped into the living room of her bungalow and could see why she had been immediately attracted to this home. Honey-colored wood floors with matching trim around the windows set off the interior. Dark crown molding lined the walls. Even though it needed work, the craftsmanship harkened back to another era. Alex's dad had taught him to appreciate the details of old homes.

Lily scanned her living room nervously. "I'm sorry things are such a mess."

LOVE AT WILD HARBOR

"Don't apologize. It's beautiful. I can see why you bought it."

"Really?" Her eyes lit up like they did in high school. "I thought all you'd see were the problems. Or maybe that's all I'm seeing after living here."

"What I see is *potential*. Good bones. It's so much harder to fix up a home that lacks that. I could see myself living in a house like this. So much better than my postage stamp apartment in California."

"Yeah, but your weather—it's probably gorgeous there right now."

"It is. But there's something about Wild Harbor that I miss, especially the seasons. I love that in the middle of May, the evenings are cool while the days are warm. I miss the leaves in fall and the snow around Christmas."

"Just wait until we get snow . . . next April. I'll start questioning why I live here."

She smiled, and he felt a surge of confidence to ask her to join them tonight.

"Speaking of living here, I wanted to hit up George's for pizza. Megan, Cassidy and Matt are all coming."

Lily's gaze dropped to the floor. "I'm not sure. I haven't even showered today. I thought I was going to paint the shop, but Megan and Cass finished it for me."

Alex sensed Lily's surprise, and he felt pleasure in knowing he had secretly contributed.

"Plus, have you seen this mess on my head?" She pointed at her disheveled bun. Stray hairs were falling out everywhere.

"We could meet in an hour if you want to get ready. Or come as you are. I don't mind."

Lily scrunched up her nose. "Really? Because I probably don't smell so great."

"I'm not letting you get out of a night of fun that easily."

"I'm not trying to get out of anything. I just have a lot to do."

"Like what?"

"Checking on my dad."

"So, we'll visit your dad first, before we get pizza."

She shook her head. "He's not like you remember him."

"Your parents were a second mom and dad to me. Remember all the times I came to your house after school?"

"My mom had to buy twice as many groceries because of all the food you ate."

"She called me her bonus son."

"I think she just felt sorry for you," Lily teased.

"She took pity on a constantly hungry teenage boy." He smiled, remembering Becky's kindness. "I'll wait around next door, and we'll stop by their house on the way to the restaurant."

"Alex, I'm not sure—"

"If you don't come, I'll have to explain things to Megan. She sent me over to make you say yes. Besides, you need to eat." He remembered her being stubborn, but this was ridiculous. He was offering her a free dinner.

Why was she resisting so much?

"Okay, I'll go—for an hour. But first, let me take a shower and call Dad."

"I have some work to finish up at the house." He turned to leave. "Come over when you're ready."

"You're going to wait in that empty house alone? That's creepy."

"No creepier than working in a chocolate shop alone."

"Okay, point taken. But you can sit next to Charlie if you need a place to hang out." She nodded toward a black and white cat lounging on top of a gray couch. The cat lifted his sleepy head and yawned as Alex sat down next to him.

"Help yourself to a drink." She walked to the hallway, calling over her shoulder. "Just don't bother raiding the pantry. It's pretty much empty except for some stale croutons and cat food."

"Mmm, cat food. Tempting."

"On second thought," she said, spinning around. "Stay away from the cat food. Didn't you eat dog food once as a kid?"

"Only because you double-dared me."

"Oh, so it's *my* fault you ate dog food?" She gave him a wry smile and headed down the hallway.

Alex watched her leave and realized how quickly they had slipped into the usual camaraderie. It was what had made them good friends back in high school. When Alex had tried to joke with other girls, his humor had always fallen flat. They either hadn't known how to take it or thought he was being critical. He had regularly failed on first dates by trying to find this same sort of chemistry.

He had learned, through a series of dating disasters, to play it straight with his dates. Don't open up too much. Just be the macho guy they expect. Strong and silent. Especially with the girls in love with the idea of dating a celebrity. Returning to Wild Harbor made him believe he could be himself again, without the celebrity status.

Lily had known him better than anyone in high school. She knew his favorite cereal. His favorite soda. Even the band he couldn't stop listening to. She knew that he loved supreme pizza with banana peppers, but couldn't stand to be near blue cheese. Despite all this, he sensed she was avoiding him, even though he still felt the chemistry they had together.

He scanned her living room pictures, mostly family on the beach and vacation photos. His eyes stopped on a high school yearbook tucked neatly into a bookshelf. He walked over and pulled it out. Their senior yearbook. He opened it and saw it was filled with signatures and well wishes.

"To the sweetest girl in the class," one signature read.

Another classmate had written in big cursive letters with

way too many hearts and exclamation points: "To my best friend, don't you ever change!!!"

Alex glanced to the bottom and found his own handwritten message: "I'm really going to miss you when you leave. Please don't forget about me."

When she'd left for college, he had worked for his dad's construction crew, taking acting classes at a local community college in the evening. Lily had come home for breaks, but it had never seemed the same. There had been something unspoken between them, a wedge in their relationship. She had moved on, with new friends and love interests.

How could he even compete?

Then his father had died of a heart attack Lily's senior year of college. She had made a special trip home for the funeral, approaching him with tears in her eyes. "I'm so sorry, Alex. I wish I could be here for you."

But you won't.

She would go back to her new friends and leave him alone to deal with his grief. That was when he had decided to pursue his dream of going to LA, and said goodbye to this small town and his dreams about Lily Woods. It was the last time he had seen her.

Reading the yearbook, he found it strangely ironic that he was the one who had left. She had returned to put down roots in Wild Harbor after graduating from college.

If he had only stayed a few more months until she had moved back, she might have given him a second chance. Now, it was too late. He didn't regret his decision, but there was an unanswered question that still plagued him.

What if he had stayed?

He clapped the yearbook shut and placed it back on the shelf. He hadn't planned for things to turn out this way, but by some divine plan, he was stuck seeing Lily every day.

He rubbed his hand across his forehead. He was in over his

head, and he knew it. *This is going to be a very long month, unless I can find a way . . .*

An idea began to roll around in his head, like a stray marble. A crazy idea that would probably never work.

If he was going to survive his trip to Wild Harbor, he needed a way to keep his feelings in check—and Lily out of the way.

CHAPTER SIX

LILY

As she looked at herself one last time in the antique mirror, she wondered what Alex thought of her. At least she looked a little more presentable than when she had arrived home. Her hair hung loosely around her shoulders, framing her face, as she swiped on lip gloss. She wasn't beautiful, not like the movie stars he was used to, but she looked like herself.

Good ol' dependable Lily. Like a used car.

Her phone buzzed with a message from Mom.

Mom: No need to stop in. Busy day at physical therapy. Dad is sleeping right now. Enjoy your time with Alex tonight. Ask him if he can come for dinner tomorrow.

She walked into the living room, where Alex sat working on something, deep in thought.

When he looked up, his eyes swept over her transformed appearance, and he smiled. "Feel better?"

"Like a new woman. It's amazing what a shower can do."

He quickly put his tablet away and stood to open the door.

She grabbed a light jacket. "It's my house. I should probably be opening up the door for you. Besides, it's not like we're on a date." As soon as she said it, she wanted to take the words back. She tried to turn the conversation away from her blunder. "By the way, Mom wanted to know if you'd come over tomorrow night for dinner. No pressure, but at some point she has to make your favorite lasagna."

"Home-cooked food? I'd love that."

"I'll let her know. Entertaining a celebrity will make her day."

He stopped outside his truck. "I don't want to be a celebrity. Just plain Alex, the kid always hanging around, eating all her food."

His smile made Lily's stomach feel funny.

Maybe it was hunger pains.

She sneaked another peek at Alex as he started the truck.

Nope.

Alex was making her react like a schoolgirl with a hopeless crush again, the last thing she wanted. He probably had dozens of women vying for his attention back in Hollywood. Lily avoided looking at him as he began to accelerate, her palms sweaty.

"I have an idea I want to propose to you," Alex said, as he focused on the road.

Lily shifted in her seat. "What is it?"

"I have no idea if the production company will approve this, so it's just an idea. I've always wanted to do a double episode where we renovate two homes at the same time. It might extend our schedule by several weeks, but I think it would save us money in travel costs, so I might be able to convince them."

"What does that have to do with me?"

Alex slowed the truck as he turned and parked behind the restaurant where the lighting was dim. He turned, and his eyes locked on hers.

"I'd like the second home to be yours, Lily."

"Mine? But why?"

"Didn't you tell me how you haven't had the time or money to renovate since you bought it?"

"Yes, but I'm planning on doing it as soon as business picks up. I've only been open four months, and I'm hoping the summer tourist season will turn things around."

"Why wait? Not only can you have it done now, I have a whole crew who can do it for you."

"But I'm not planning on selling my home."

"I won't make that part of the deal. They either need to allow you to stay after the renovation, or we won't do it."

"I don't know what to say, Alex. That's incredibly generous, but there's no way I can do it."

"Why not?"

"Because I want to be part of the renovation. To prove to myself I can do it."

Alex paused.

Lily sensed he was grasping for Plan B.

"Okay, so what if that's part of the agreement? You can help the crew a few times, as long as you're okay with being on TV. An opportunity like this will never come around ever again."

Lily looked at Alex, the cut of his jaw in the streetlight, apprehension and excitement swirling in her mind. She didn't want to let Alex back into her life so easily. He would see how desperate she was for help, and she had her heart set on fixing up her place with Dad. Yet, how could she turn his amazing offer down? This would solve a huge problem. It would be years before she saved enough money for this project. Alex's crew could finish it faster without the inevitable headaches she would face as a beginner. More than anything, she wanted to make it possible to move her parents in with her.

"Alex, I'm willing. But I don't even know how to thank you."

"You can always pay me in food," he teased, grinning that boyish smile she remembered so well.

"You mean chocolate?"

"That works too. There's only one catch. You'd need to move in with your parents until the project is done."

"That would give me the chance to help Dad, as long as I can make final decisions about colors, the design, and what I want left untouched. If this is the best way—"

"It's the only way," he said quickly.

She opened the door to step out and wondered why Alex was doing this. Did he feel sorry for her? Or was this just to make up for the falling-out that happened their senior year?

As they walked into George's, the smell of fresh baked dough and spicy sausage filled the room with an irresistible aroma. An eruption of cheers sounded from a back booth where the gang waited.

"The star has arrived," Matt announced, scooting closer to Cameron so they could make room for Alex. "It's about time."

Alex gave him a look. "No need to make room. I'm good." He grabbed a chair, flipped it around backward, and sat down.

Lily slid next to Cassidy and Megan.

"What took you guys so long?" Megan asked as she grabbed another sip of soda.

"Sorry, my fault," Lily said. "I needed a shower after work."

"Don't tell me you were going to work all night again." Cassidy put her hand on Lily's arm.

"No, I didn't have to. I completed my next chocolate order and even prepped some chocolates for the grand opening. By the way, I was shocked to see my shop was totally painted. How did you girls finish so fast?"

A look passed between her siblings who both smiled and averted their eyes.

"What can I say?" Megan beamed. "We're just *that* good."

"That's not the whole story. I can see it in your eyes." Lily turned to Alex.

He was staring intently at the menu, smirking. Matt was doing the same thing.

"What are you smiling about?" Lily pulled Alex's menu away. "I was trying to thank my sisters, and you clowns are ruining the moment."

"It's nothing."

"No, it's not. I can tell. Is there a private joke going on?"

Alex grabbed his menu back. "Matt is kicking me under the table. Just like old times."

Lily looked at Cassidy. "Will they ever stop being junior high boys?"

"I don't think so."

"Hey, I heard that!" Matt pointed at his sisters.

Cameron rested his arms on the table. "Alex, what's the update on the show? You've secured a location, but it's top secret, right?"

"Uh, not anymore." Alex looked at Lily. "I'm going to be Lily's neighbor for the next month."

"No way," Cam said. "How did that happen?"

"His crew was blocking my driveway, so I went over to tell them to move."

"Not exactly the welcome you were hoping for." Cam patted Alex on the shoulder. He turned back to Lily. "If Alex is going to be next door, you should get on set as an extra and beef up your home renovation skills."

"She might be involved." Alex gave Lily a knowing smile. "If things work out."

"What do you mean?" Megan leaned on the table, eyeing them both.

"I'm trying to land a deal for Lily's house. A double episode where we renovate two homes"

"What?" Cassidy exclaimed.

"I can't believe it. Your very own fixer-upper." Megan squeezed Lily's hand.

"It's not official yet," Lily added. "Alex hasn't even presented the idea, but it would be a dream come true if they say yes."

"Hey, can you come to my house next?" Matt asked.

"Sorry man, Lily's house and the one next door are all I can manage."

Alex stood. "Enough about work. Who's ready for some pinball?"

Matt and Cam joined Alex, leaving the girls in their booth waiting for their order while a twangy country tune echoed in the background.

Cassidy took a sip of her water. "What are the odds that Alex's TV show would pick the house next to yours?"

Megan lifted her eyebrows. "Almost strangely coincidental, don't you think?"

"What do you mean?" Lily asked.

"Whether he arranged it or it was an act of God, it seems too good to be true."

"He didn't arrange it. I saw the look on his face when he realized I was the neighbor. He was shocked."

Megan gave Lily a look. "I think it's a strange coincidence that he ended up next door, of all places. Almost like it was *meant to be*."

"Why is that so strange? It's not like we'll see each other much. I would have to move out during the renovation. I would hardly see him."

"Uh-huh. Right." Megan wiggled her eyebrows at her sister.

"What?" Lily knew there was something to her sister's tone.

"He wanted to date you back in high school. How convenient that he's right next door."

Lily shook her head. "We were only friends. That's it." Lily looked at Cassidy for support. "Tell her, Cass. We were *friends*."

Cassidy's eyes softened. "Lily, when you left for college, Alex was crushed. He talked about you all the time."

"He was lonely. Besides, the last thing I need is a guy to complicate things. In a few weeks, he's heading back, and I'll still be here, trying to get my business off the ground."

Megan took another swig of her soda. "I can see it all over your face when you look at him. Just like high school."

"See what?" Lily touched her cheeks, suddenly aware of how flushed they were.

"You still feel something for him."

"I do *not*. Just because I had a crush on him in high school does not mean I have feelings now. Alex is a nice guy, but there's no future for us." Even as Lily said the words, it echoed back as a hollow promise.

If her sisters knew how she felt, how could she hide it from Alex? *How can I conceal my feelings the entire time he's here?*

She avoided her sisters' eyes and glanced around. Her parent's neighbors ate salad a few tables over, and nearby a family from church waited for their food with four small kids who restlessly wiggled in their seats. Suddenly, she felt the gaze of someone in the room. A face locked on hers.

Her eyes flitted across the room to a pale face tucked in the corner. Her breath caught for a moment. *Thomas.*

How did he know she was here? Had he followed her?

He didn't even live in Wild Harbor, but was from a neighboring town about twenty minutes away. He lifted his hand, a tiny wave that no one but her could see.

Her eyes darted away from him as she looked down at her silverware. About a year ago, she had felt pressure to find someone before she turned thirty, as if that magic number signaled she was too old to still be single. How silly she was to think there was some great disparity between twenty-nine and thirty.

Then she'd met Thomas at an outdoor party her best friend,

Sadie, had thrown for the Fourth of July. Lily and Thomas had been the only two single people without dates, which had made it inevitable that by the end of the night they would be sitting alone at a patio table while everyone else gathered on lawn blankets for fireworks. They'd polished off their ice cream while sharing funny stories from their past under the crack and sizzle of bottle rockets and firecrackers.

Before he'd left that night, he had asked for her phone number. That was the beginning of their romance, which at first had been mostly all the good parts of a new relationship—flowers and nice restaurants, laughter and lingering at tables long into the night. But after a few months, little cracks had appeared in their relationship, growing into irreparable fissures that had eroded her trust in Thomas. He would snap at her for no reason or get mad about seemingly minor mistakes.

She'd begun to feel like she was walking on eggshells every time she was around him. It had been exhausting, to say the least.

When she'd dumped him six months ago, she'd thought that ended things. And for a few months it had. Until he started texting, leaving apologies on the phone, or sending random messages about his day. She hadn't thought it odd at the time, but she was also so absorbed in running her shop and helping her parents that she hadn't bothered responding.

Suddenly, her phone buzzed in her purse. She picked it up to study the screen while Megan and Cassidy took bets on which of the guys would win the pinball game.

Her stomach sank as she saw the message was from Thomas.

Thomas: Funny running into you here of all places! Remember when we went out for pizza together? We should do lunch soon. Not to pry, but are you on a date with someone tonight? You look beautiful.

45

Lily chewed the corner of her lip as she typed.

Lily: I'm not on a date. But please stop texting me.

She debated whether or not to tell her sisters about Thomas or to ignore him completely and hope he got the message. Surely, it was just a coincidence he was here. To her dismay, he continued to glare at her from the corner booth as she shifted uncomfortably.

"The guys must have finished their game," Megan said, before lowering her voice to Lily. "Did you see the way Alex kept looking over here? It's like he can't keep his eyes off you."

The heat crept up Lily's neck. She hadn't noticed because she had been too worried about her creepy ex-boyfriend being in the room. Between her attraction to Alex and Thomas's disconcerting presence, she wished she had just stayed home and binged a TV series.

As the guys returned to their table, Lily avoided Alex's eyes, opting to concentrate on the ice floating in her drink. She stirred the straw in circles as her cheeks flushed hotter, constricting her breathing and causing her to feel light-headed.

"Excuse me, I need to go to the restroom." She left the table in a hurry, a wave of emotion hurtling over her. In the bathroom, she locked the one-person stall and leaned back against the door as beads of sweat formed on her forehead.

Thomas had shown up without warning. Alex Briggs was home. And Lily had no idea what she was going to do about either one.

CHAPTER SEVEN

ALEX

The next morning, as he took a long walk on the beach to clear his head, he sensed that Lily had been avoiding him last night. Had he said something offensive?

She had averted her eyes for the rest of the night at George's, her initial warmth replaced by something like coldness.

When he'd driven her home, she'd stared out the window and given an excuse about how she was too tired to talk. Her face was clouded, like a stormy spring day.

Leave her alone, man. This was what you wanted, right? Distance between you and her.

After showering and throwing on a T-shirt and jeans, he drove to Lily's and sat outside, ready to work up a proposal for her home renovation. His job was simple. Persuade his boss to say yes. Picking up his phone, he texted her a quick note.

Alex: Are you up? I'm bringing doughnuts. Your favorite.
Lily: How do you know my favorite?

Alex: You don't remember the jelly doughnut incident? Plus, I need to take measurements for Project Top Secret.

He knocked on the door and waited, holding the plain white box. When she opened the door, dressed in a white blouse and jeans, her long hair swept over one shoulder, he almost forgot why he was there.

"Hey." He tried not to stare, though he couldn't help himself. A beautiful woman stood before him, and he was fully aware of it every time he was near her.

Alex looked down, afraid she could read his mind. "Your personal doughnut delivery man, at your service." He handed her the box.

Lily slowly opened the lid. "Apple fritters from The Doughnut Shop? These are my favorite!" She shut the lid quickly and narrowed her eyes. "Who told you?"

"Nobody told me. I remembered—that one summer when you were working at the Snack Shack on the beach? I brought you doughnuts when you opened your shift. One time I made the mistake of bringing you a jelly doughnut. *Never* again."

"Was I a jerk about it? I'm so sorry."

"You gave me a hard time, and I never forgot your favorite after that."

"Well, then I forgive you, especially since you only gave me ten minutes notice before coming over."

"I'm an early riser, in case you didn't notice."

"I did and won't hold it against you . . . *this* time."

"Hmm, maybe I should send a five a.m. wake-up text next time."

"Not funny." She stepped aside to let him in and led him to the kitchen. "I did just make hot coffee, if you want some." She poured a cup and started scarfing down a doughnut while standing at the counter.

"That would be great." He looked around. "Do you want to

sit down to eat?" He pointed to the table piled with mail, magazines, an open book, and a few dirty mugs.

"If you can't tell, I never eat there. I probably should start packing if you're going to be working here."

She moved the piles to a spare box, and then grabbed another cup of coffee and two plates.

"Do you actually use those plates? I mean, since you don't use your table?" He gave her a teasing smile.

"Of course I do. Most of the time. That is, if I'm not eating out." She smiled guiltily. "Don't judge. I have a business to run and my dad to help with. Most days I skip lunch. It's just easier."

"No judgment from me. I usually eat alone in hotels. For my stay in Wild Harbor, I rented a condo on the north side of town, but I still don't have anyone to eat with. Dining with someone is a treat. The company, the conversation, the food. Even if it is doughnuts." He took a bite of his apple fritter and put the rest on his plate.

"I never thought about that before. What about when you're home—surely you have friends you eat with?"

"Yeah, but life in LA is different. Fast-paced. A hustle-all-the-time vibe. Sometimes, I grab a meal with a friend, but I still eat alone more than I'd like to." Although he didn't say it, he missed dining with a woman. The chance to savor a meal and engage in deep conversation was one of his favorite things. He hadn't realized what an incredible pleasure it was until he lost it. "Lately, I've really missed Wild Harbor. I made a list of all the places I want to visit while I'm here. The beach. Your family. The cemetery."

"It's been eight years since your dad died, hasn't it?"

He nodded. "Being here has made me realize how much I've missed this place. My friends. You." He stopped and looked at her.

Their eyes locked.

She glanced away from him as she rose. "Did you want any cream or sugar for your coffee?"

"No, I'm good."

At the counter, she poured more cream into her coffee. "I figured you had plenty of friends in California."

"I have friends, but not like you or the guys from high school. There's something special about the people you grew up with. I met one girl in California who reminded me of home. We were both in an acting class and started dating. We were cast in this terrible play together, and she kept cracking me up every time I'd step offstage. She reminded me of you . . ." He stopped, unable to say more. He had promised himself he would keep this part of his life separate, like a carefully hidden gift. "Coming back to Wild Harbor made me realize how much I've missed it."

Lily walked back to the table and sat in her chair. "I didn't know you felt that way."

"I haven't told anyone else. Which is why I want to make the most of my visit here—starting with your house. I need as much evidence as possible when I present my case about renovating your home."

"Where should we start, then?"

"How about in here?" He stood, took a final swig of coffee, and pulled out his measuring tape. As he began measuring the kitchen, he noticed how many things needed work in her home. The ceramic tile was cracked in the kitchen. Trim pieces had come loose on the wall. A closet door hung crooked. Broken door handles. Lights that no longer worked. Windowpanes that were cracked. The house was falling apart in a million little ways, and all he wanted to do was fix it for her.

"Do you have some tools around here?"

"I've got a hammer. What are you going to start with?"

"Well, this trim for one. I could put a quick finishing nail in there and reattach it to the wall."

"Can I do it? I know you're the expert, but I really want to learn."

He looked at the expectation in her eyes and couldn't say no.

She grabbed a hammer from a kitchen drawer. "I wanted this house to be a project Dad and I worked on together. My dream was to have him teach me, but I don't know if he'll ever be able to walk, let alone use a power tool. If I'm going to live here, I need to learn how to do this." She gripped the hammer tightly, her eyes pleading for him to say yes.

The last thing he'd do was say no to her.

"I'd love to." He took the hammer, and his hand grazed hers. In that brief touch, he wanted something more.

He shouldn't get himself tangled up in this. *Or her.* But every time he brushed by her or she smiled at him, something held him there, a desire he didn't want to let go of. He could really fall for her, but something kept pulling him back, reminding him he was treading on dangerous ground.

Lily brought out some nails. "Do these look right?

"Those will work. I'll hold this piece in place." He handed her the hammer and positioned the trim where it had fallen off. "You place the nail here. Hold the nail steady and give it a good smack."

Lily stood next to him, holding the tiny nail and lifting the hammer. "Am I going to hit my finger with this? It's so small."

She was holding the nail wrong, so he took the hammer back. "You're going to be in pain if you hold it like that. Let me show you."

As Alex reached to show her how to grasp the nail, he leaned over her shoulder, his hand touching hers. He smelled the scent of her shampoo, as he wrapped his other hand around the hammer with hers. With his arms around her, his heart began to beat faster.

"Like this?" she said quietly, staring at their hands.

"Now, carefully take your first swing, and aim for the top of the nail." He guided her hand as she carefully swung the hammer.

She tapped the nail slowly at first, then gained confidence as the nail sank into place.

He let go as she finished pounding it in. "You did it."

"With your help. I'm amazed I didn't smash my fingers." She turned to him and looked up into his eyes. "Thank you."

Alex was still next to her, close enough he could run his hand across her cheek. Their eyes locked. A yearning in his chest tightened his breathing, making him feel things he'd not felt in a long time.

She looked away and took a step back.

"Is there something wrong?"

Lily shook her head. "No."

"Because last night, I could have sworn you were trying to avoid me."

She looked back at him again and a shadow passed over her eyes. "Not avoid you. I just need to remember why you're here. Your job. My home."

"Yes, *that*. But I should've told you how nice it will be to have a friend on set."

"A friend?" She walked away, and he wondered if she felt the spark of something more between them. "Sure, I guess."

"Because if we're going to work on your house, I need your cooperation."

She faced him. "And I need you to teach me, so that after you leave, I can do things on my own. It needs to be part of the agreement."

"I'm not sure how much the production company will allow you to do. I'm submitting the proposal this morning, but there are rules—"

"But you're the star, so you can teach me even when we're not on camera, right?"

The way she looked at him, her eyes filled with expectation, made him want to give in. "I'll teach you what I can."

"I'm willing to learn, even if it means smashing my thumb."

"I'll help you avoid that as much as I can. So, what's next?"

"Let me grab my long list of repairs." She ran off to the other room.

Alex took a deep breath. He had promised to help, but he knew better than to let himself get too involved with her. If his plan received approval, he hoped the production company would put some restrictions on Lily's involvement. He needed a way to keep his feelings in check.

Move on, mister.

LATER THAT DAY, after he'd sent his proposal to his producer and had written down Lily's long list of repairs, Alex checked his phone. A new email from Phil appeared in his inbox:

Alex,

I love the idea of the double episode with the home next door. I ran it by the others, and they all agreed. So, we're green lighting this for you ASAP. Extend your stay in Wild Harbor to six weeks. Also, we want the girl in this episode (Lily, I think?). We need to hear her story, see her on camera, experience the chemistry between you two—you as her mentor. Let's draw out the human-interest part of this. I know you can keep things professional between you and her.

-Phil

Alex shut his phone off and jammed it into his pocket. He had counted on them saying no to Lily's involvement in the project or at least restricting her. The whole reason he had come up with this plan was to keep her out of the way and his feelings at bay. Now, his plan had backfired. Not only had he agreed to help her with home repairs, she would be on set working with him for part of the renovation process.

Alex ran his fingers through his hair. He needed this project to go well. To ignore this thing between them. It might be next to impossible, but he knew one thing for sure: he couldn't fall for Lily Woods.

CHAPTER EIGHT

LILY

S he hadn't expected to hear from Alex yet. So, when she saw a text giving her the news, she felt a mixture of excitement and worry.

Alex: They like the idea of your home renovation. Still working out details, but they want you to be a part of the filming. Let's talk later.

Lily hated the idea of being on camera. She had no yearnings for fame, but the thought of working on her home with Alex filled her with something she had not felt in a long time: hope that things in her life could turn around.

As Alex spent the rest of the week working on the home next door, Lily caught glimpses of him and was embarrassed at how much she reverted to the giddy, awkward girl from high school. Feelings surfaced that she had thought long buried after everything had gone horribly wrong with Thomas. Alex brought out something dormant in her. She had forgotten what longing felt like.

Focus, girl. These feelings are nothing but a distraction.

Right now, she needed to keep her chocolate shop from closing. Although she had opened just four months ago, the business had floundered. Tucked away on a side street, a small shop between an empty storefront and a dog groomer's, she wasn't exactly in prime real estate territory. Although Lily always had possessed a love for making chocolates, she had only pursued her hobby for friends and family before quitting her job. Now that she was dedicated full-time, business was slowly trickling in, but many people in Wild Harbor still didn't know she existed. Even the grand opening seemed like a last-ditch attempt to salvage her business and, in some ways, her life.

Her whole world was built like a house of cards. If one thing fell, it would all fall. The prospect of Alex's offer to renovate her home shone like a single ray of light across a heavily clouded sky.

Her shoulders tense, she took a deep breath as she walked into her shop. Just last week, her mom had told her, "You don't have to hold it all together or worry about the future. That's what faith is for."

She had bristled under her mom's simple explanations. She had wanted to believe it would be that easy. That she could just pass off her worries like passing a plate of salad around the table. But nothing about faith came easily, especially when things were going badly.

"Well, that's all good when things are going well," she told her mom. "But what about when they aren't?"

Lily's faith had slumped recently under the weight of her problems. Not that she had abandoned it, but rather she was trying to understand it. She had mistakenly believed the myth that she would not suffer if she took the right steps, made good choices, and treated everyone with kindness. But as her life had begun to crumble, she'd realized that being "right" and "kind" had nothing to do with it. She wasn't in control. Now that she was facing one hurdle after another, she understood how much harder it was to hang on to faith when nothing was going right.

Her thoughts were interrupted by the bell on the door as Edna Long entered. Edna, who had retired early after a long stint as a teacher, was a regular buyer, stopping by every few weeks for her ladies' teatime group. She wore a loose, yellow floral blouse that billowed in the breeze and only accentuated her large frame. Lily suspected Edna Long was probably eating as many chocolates as she was serving at her parties.

"Lily, dear, hello. I just dropped Peaches off at the grooming salon, and I thought I'd stop in for another order of truffles."

Lily smiled. Peaches was the beloved Pekingese pup who had kept Edna company since her husband died. She treated her like a baby, dressing her up with doggie bows and sparkly collars.

"You're in luck. I made some yesterday. Thelma hasn't bought me out yet." Thelma also had a weakness for chocolate and small pets (something she noted in her dating app profile) but, unlike Edna, was as skinny as a rail.

"Oh, good. I'll have to rub it in." Edna smiled as she touched her curled hair, which billowed like a cloud above her head. She had a regular appointment at the beauty salon every week and somehow managed to keep her hairdo looking exactly the same between visits.

"Oh, have you heard the news?" Edna's eyes sparkled with juicy gossip. "Alex Briggs is going to make Wild Harbor the star of his show."

"Yes, I heard." Lily tried to hide a smile as she filled a bag with truffles. Not only did she know the news, it was happening right next door. If she told Edna, the whole town would know.

Edna leaned in as if she were sharing a piece of juicy gossip. "There's a house next to my cousin's that's in desperate need of renovation, not to mention a few others in my neighborhood."

"I heard they've selected a home."

"You're kidding! Have you seen Alex around yet?" Edna's eyes sparkled.

Lily blushed and turned away from Edna as she boxed the truffles. "Yes, I've seen him." She glanced back at Edna, whose mouth hung open.

"You've seen him . . . like *in person*? Well, aren't you a lucky girl! Did you get his autograph?"

If Edna knew that Alex had wrapped his arms around her and showed her how to hit a nail, she'd probably faint. "I didn't ask for his autograph. Would you like me to get one for you?"

Edna's eyes almost bulged out of her sockets. "Would I ever! You know I'd be a customer for life if you did that."

Lily laughed and handed Edna her order. "I can't promise Alex will do it, but I'd be happy to ask him. Just for you."

Edna took the chocolates and handed Lily cash with the exact change. She was one of the few customers who always had the right amount, down to the penny.

"I saw you are having a grand opening in a few weeks. Maybe you should ask Alex to attend. You'd get loads of people here for it."

The idea had never occurred to Lily, but she knew Edna was right. If Alex came, so would half of Wild Harbor, and that would mean a big bump in sales for her shop.

"I'm sure his schedule is really busy. We'll have to see."

"I'd come if he was here. I bet Thelma would too."

Lily laughed. "I never knew you were such a big fan of Alex's."

"Have you seen him on the show? He makes a T-shirt look good." Then she laughed at herself, took her chocolates, and headed for the door. "Don't forget to ask him!" She called over her shoulder as the bell jingled and she stepped outside.

Edna's idea could change everything. The grand opening

would pull more people in if she offered some kind of a draw. And Alex was definitely an attraction.

But would he do it?

Lily didn't want to ask for a favor, especially to use his celebrity for her shop. But she was desperate. She needed this event to boost her sales and secure her reputation in the community.

Alex was already doing so much for her. How could she ask him for more?

CHAPTER NINE

LILY

As Lily spent the morning crafting dark chocolate truffles, she fell into her usual rhythm of chocolate-making, stirring the melted chocolate until it turned into a glossy river of deep brown. She kept trying to avoid thinking of Alex, but their moment in the house kept resurfacing. She could really fall for him if she let herself . . . *not that she could let herself.* Therein . . . was the problem.

Just then, she heard her phone beep and glanced down to see a text.

Alex: I know you like tacos almost as much as chocolate. Even though you don't eat lunch, I'm officially asking you to eat lunch with me. Plus, I have news about your house.
Lily: Tacos? YES!

She set aside the truffles and walked to the sink to clean up. Before she could even finish drying her hands, the bell on the door rang.

"How did you get here so quickly?" she asked, expecting to hear Alex's familiar voice. Turning to greet him, she stopped. "Thomas."

Her smile suddenly faded as she stood frozen in place. The last time she had been alone with him, things had gone badly. A sickening feeling erupted in her stomach.

"Expecting someone else?" He stepped to the counter.

"What are you doing here?" Her tone held an edge. She stayed glued in her spot next to the sink, gripping the paper towel tightly.

"Haven't been in here before. Thought I would see how you were. I noticed you didn't respond to my texts."

"I'm fine." She threw the towel in the trash, feeling suddenly jittery. She wished she wasn't alone with him, having this conversation. Why hadn't she locked the door after Edna left? It might be awhile before Alex, or anyone for that matter, would come.

"You know, I was thinking about you the other day." A shadow crossed his face. The way he said it made her stomach turn. "Missing old times together. I wondered if you wanted to go out for lunch."

"I already have plans today." She crossed her arms, glancing at the door to check if anyone was coming in.

"Then how about another day . . . maybe tomorrow?" He seemed almost desperate to set a date.

"Listen, Thomas, I'm really busy with work and my dad's health issues right now."

"I heard about his stroke. Is he any better?"

She looked down at the ground and shifted her weight. "He's not as far along as he'd like." She wished he would leave, but he seemed hesitant, like he wanted to say something. "Why are you here, Thomas?"

Although he texted and called her, he hadn't talked to her alone since she had broken things off months ago. When she had first started dating him, she hadn't known him to be the type who had a temper that snapped like a brittle twig. She remembered the time she'd dropped the container of blueberries while unloading groceries. They had scattered across the floor like marbles.

"Why are you so clumsy?" he had yelled at her.

At the time, it had seemed like a slip, the undercurrent of irritation flaring in his face. But she remembered how it had jarred her, hurting like the tiniest of paper cuts. Each time he had grown angry with her, it had sliced open another painful cut, until she'd felt like she was dying of a thousand paper cuts.

"I just wanted you to know that I'm sorry about what happened to your dad."

"Well, thanks." She looked in his eyes, and for a second, she believed him. He didn't seem like a person who held his anger inside until it boiled over into something raw and ugly. Few people knew that side of Thomas. Even fewer knew the damage it had done to her.

"I wish things hadn't ended like they did between us."

Even as he said it, her shoulders tensed.

He started to walk around the counter, where she stood frozen in place.

A panic rose up inside as he drew near.

The bell on the door rang again.

Lily looked up to see Alex striding through the door with a take-out box of tacos in his arms.

Thomas stopped, then stepped away.

Relief flooded Lily's body. "I'm sorry, Thomas. I can't talk right now." Her gaze fixed on Alex.

Alex set the tacos on a table nearby, eyeing Thomas.

She scooted by Thomas and walked to her childhood friend. "Alex, so glad you're here. Have you met Thomas?"

"Uh, no." He turned to Thomas and put his hand out. "Hi, I'm Alex."

Thomas shook his hand, and a realization passed over his face. "Wait a minute. You're that guy from TV. The one who used to live here." He looked at Lily. "How do you know him?"

"We were friends from school. He lived just a few houses down from me."

Thomas looked at the carryout and glanced from Alex to Lily.

"I'm making sure Lily eats lunch while trying to catch up on the last eight years," Alex said. "A lot of time has passed."

"Yeah, it has." Thomas's voice had an edge of coldness.

She could tell he didn't like this arrangement, not that he could do anything about it. Whatever he had planned on saying to her would have to wait.

"Bye, Thomas." She gave him a look that indicated his time here was over.

Thomas turned and slowly walked out the door.

Alex opened the boxes and set out the chips and salsa. "He didn't seem very pleased you were having lunch with me." He motioned for Lily to sit across from him.

"He wasn't. Not at all." She sank into her chair and exhaled. She hadn't realized how afraid she had been until now. "We're not exactly on good terms since I broke things off six months ago."

"Oh?" He handed her a soft taco. "Anything that a taco can't fix?"

She smiled. He always did know how to relieve the tension. "If tacos could fix this, I'd be a happy woman. But I don't want to bore you with my dating disasters."

"I spent all of high school listening to your dating stories. And I never told a soul. If it makes you feel better, I'll share my abysmal dates."

"There's no way your dating life is as bad as mine." She shook her head.

"Try me." He lifted his eyebrows in a challenge.

"You go first." She was reluctant to tell Alex what had really happened between her and Thomas. Even though they had been best friends in high school, she couldn't help but feel that Alex would think less of her if he knew the truth.

"Okay," he said. "I once went out with a woman who was dating three guys at the same time, and I didn't have a clue. When I finally confronted her, she claimed I was the one who had been unfaithful and broke things off. Then she put a fake story about me all over the Internet . . . even though I hadn't been on a date with anyone else that entire year."

"Oh, that's rough. What did you do?"

"Nothing. At that point, there wasn't a whole lot I could do. The gossip websites picked up on it, but I didn't have a TV show yet, so it died out pretty quickly. I knew her lies would eventually catch up with her. A few months later, a story broke about her rampant history of cheating after two of her boyfriends found out about each other."

"Yikes. I guess that cleared your name."

"Yep, pretty much. What about you?"

"I broke things off with Thomas right around the time I quit my job. It didn't end well."

"So, why did he stop in today?"

"I'm not sure. He seemed like he wanted to tell me something. Anyway, it's complicated."

Alex poured hot sauce on his taco. "Do you think he regrets breaking up?"

"He regrets a lot of things. How he treated me, for one. I'm just so glad you came in when you did." She took a bite of taco and avoided Alex's gaze.

Alex paused. "Is there something I should know about this guy? The look in your eyes when I walked in . . . well, let's just say I've never seen you look so relieved."

"I was." She wrestled with whether to say anything more. "Thomas is . . . how should I say it? A volatile guy. I didn't know that when I started dating him. He has an anger problem that he hides pretty well until you get to know him."

"Wait a minute." Alex stopped eating and looked at Lily, a fire in his eyes she hadn't seen before. "Does he make you feel unsafe?"

"Yeah. I guess you could say that." She fiddled with her tacos. "This is already so hard for me to talk about. Maybe we should change the subject."

He shook his head. "Lily, no man should ever make a woman feel unsafe." His eyes were locked on hers.

"I know," she whispered as she looked down, the tears welling up. "I shouldn't have told you all this. It was too much, too soon."

He reached out and touched the side of her face with the palm of his hand. "No, it wasn't too much. If you ever need me to come again, I will. In a second."

"How's that going to work when you're in California?" She'd meant it as a joke, but he didn't say anything in response. She wiped her mouth with a napkin and waved her hand. "Don't worry about me. I have my whole family here. Besides, I don't think Thomas is a threat anymore. Let's talk about something else. Like how good these tacos are." She took a bite and closed her eyes. "Chocolate might be my favorite, but tacos are a close second."

"When you told me you don't eat lunch, I decided that needed to be remedied. Not only so you can make this shop a success, but also because your dad needs you."

"You sound just like my parents."

"Hey, I'm just trying to take care of you."

She shook her head. "I don't need taking care of. But thank you anyway. How's the house project going?"

"We've hit a few snags, but they haven't been major. Good news. In between things, I received a message from Phil. They approved the entire budget for your house."

"What? You're kidding me!"

"They told me they thought it was a great idea as long as I kept things within the budget I proposed. And if you're willing, they want to feature your story."

"Oh, okay. Well . . . I guess." Lily shifted in her seat. "Not that I love being on camera. But I'll do it. What's the timeline look like?"

"They're giving me six weeks, but I can hire more crew if needed. It's going to be a tight schedule, but I think we can do it."

"Oh, my goodness, that means I'm going to be renovating a house while I'm trying to pull off my grand opening. I hadn't put that together."

"Is that a problem?" He snagged a napkin at the counter and peeked at the display case. "If so, I can help at night."

Lily smirked. "You want to help make chocolate? I don't think so. You just said you're on a tight schedule."

"Making chocolate is not like renovating a house."

"It's a lot harder than you think."

"Try me."

"With one caveat. If your chocolates don't turn out, you buy them. I can't sell them."

"Okay, fair enough." He took another bite of his taco.

"I do have one request." Lily paused and tucked some hair behind her ear. "A client of mine said I should invite you to my grand opening." She looked at him nervously and shifted her feet under the table. "I feel so uncomfortable asking, but she really wants to meet you. Plus, she said it would be good for business." Lily cringed, feeling bad she was using Alex's celebrity status. "If you don't want to do it, it's totally okay with me."

"No, Lily. I'd love to help. If you want me to be here, I'll do it."

She shook her head. "It's asking too much."

"It's not. Whatever I can do to help you, I will." He put his hand over hers.

A brief flutter stirred inside her. She swallowed her emotions so he wouldn't see how much this affected her.

"You don't have to do this," she said.

"By the look in your eyes, I can tell you want to talk me out of it, but I'm not letting you. I'll be there. Case closed."

In his resolve, she sensed there was no hope in fighting this battle. Already she had lost.

CHAPTER TEN

ALEX

The next day, Alex could barely keep his mind on his work all afternoon. Normally, he was laser-focused, checking off his to-do list, ticking every box: one, two, three.

Infuriatingly, he couldn't seem to harness his mind any more than a person could tame a wild horse. He wasn't going to allow Thomas to come near Lily again. At least, not if he could help it.

Even after she opened up to him, a space remained between them. One moment she was looking at him a certain way, and the next she'd pull away, her expression closed, like she was walling him off.

"Alex? Hey, Alex . . ."

He heard the voice of one of his crew members and looked up to see Mike standing on a ladder nearby, hoisting a piece of lumber.

"I'm sorry, Mike. I didn't hear you."

"I can tell. Especially since you almost walked into this two-by-four. You all right today?"

"Yeah, just lost in thought." *Was it that obvious?*

"You're the guy usually keeping us on track. Everything okay?"

"Oh, I'm fine. I've been distracted, that's all."

"Lemme guess—girl problems?"

Alex laughed and fidgeted with his clipboard. "Not problems, exactly. But how'd you guess?"

Mike crawled down from the ladder and joined Alex. The burly man had a full beard and wide shoulders. Not the type that looked like a ladies' man. "I don't know. A guy like you suddenly can't focus? I just put two and two together. So, who's the lucky girl?"

"We're not together." Alex glanced around to see if anyone was listening. "Have you met Lily from next door?"

"I've seen her. The short blonde who was spittin' fire when we parked our trailer in her drive?"

"That's her."

"Good luck, man." Mike patted Alex's shoulder and chuckled. "It's about time after Trina."

Alex shook his head. "That's the thing. She'd never consider it. Too much history between us."

"Only one way to find out—ask her."

Alex took off his construction hat and wiped his forehead. "I think I'd be better off staying away."

"Come on, man, what do you have to lose?"

"More than you know. Besides, I'm not her type."

Mike shrugged. "Like I said, only one way to find out." Mike picked up his ladder and strode away, leaving Alex standing alone.

It's one dinner with her family, Alex told himself as he drove through town to pick up Lily. *I can survive this.*

As he passed the floral shop on Main Street, he remembered

Becky Woods had always loved flowers. Her gardens had earned her the Yard of the Month award in Wild Harbor several times when he was a kid. He made a quick U-turn, then parked next to a huge plate glass window, where a slender woman with short, graying hair was assembling a bouquet.

His dad had bought flowers for his mom from this shop dozens of times during his childhood, and he could still remember his father's words of advice when they pulled up to the door. "Son, if you want a girl to stay with you for the long haul, then you do everything in your power to show her you love her."

Alex smiled at the memory of his mom's face when he had presented the flowers. He wasn't fooling anyone. Mom had thanked Alex then given Dad a wink as she put them in a vase of water.

As he entered the cramped shop, he was walloped by the overpowering fragrance of flowers.

"Can I help you?" The woman said before doing a double take and dropping the rose she was cutting. "Well, I'll be . . . you're that TV guy." She didn't even notice her flower on the floor.

Alex held back a grin. "I was hoping to buy two bouquets of flowers."

She stared, chomping on a piece of gum, her jaw working like a llama's. She put her hand on her hip and gazed at Alex. A tiny whistle escaped from her lips as she shook her head in disbelief. "You gotta be pulling my chain. Is this one of those practical jokes for TV? Alex Briggs in my shop?"

"No, it's not a joke. I'm fixing up a house in town."

"Well, you could've fooled me. What can I help you with, honey?" She wiped her hands on her apron.

"I wanted to buy two bouquets of flowers."

"I got some pretty ones there." She pointed to a refrigerated case near him, still chomping her gum.

"I'll take these two," he said, pulling out two mixed floral bouquets of roses, lilies, and irises.

"Can I take a selfie with you before you go?" the woman asked as he paid. She pulled out her cell phone before Alex even answered. "My name's Pammy, by the way. Feel free to come by anytime. If you have a special someone you need flowers for, we'd love to help," she said, grinning and chomping.

She leaned over the counter toward him while she took the picture. "Well, aren't you a sweetheart." She looked at the selfie before he walked out the door. "My daughter is never gonna let me live this down."

WHEN ALEX ARRIVED at Lily's, she looked at the flowers, then back at Alex. "What is this?"

"For you." He held out the flowers. Lily was dressed in a long, flowing dress that had wowed Alex the minute she opened the door.

"They're beautiful, but what for?"

"Does it have to be for anything?"

She took them reluctantly. "That was . . . unexpected. But you know who would appreciate them even more? My mom."

"I already have a bouquet for her."

"You know the way to impress women. Let me put these in water."

He stepped inside her house as she pulled a vase out of a cabinet.

She turned suddenly. "What are you thinking about? You're smiling."

"I was just noticing how nice you look. I don't usually see you dressed up like this."

"Oh, I know. I don't dress up when I work because I'd smear melted chocolate all over the place." She glanced down at the jeans he was wearing. "Maybe I should wear jeans since you are."

"Please don't. I think you look beautiful." Even as he said it, she blushed for a moment and turned away.

"Should we go?" She headed out the door ahead of Alex. They walked toward his truck as Lily avoided his gaze. "I need to prepare you for tonight. I don't know if you realize how much my dad has changed. I don't want you to be shocked. He isn't quite like he used to be."

Alex nodded. "That must be so hard for your mom."

"He still can't walk well, so getting around the house is difficult. It's really hard to watch, but I know everyone is looking forward to catching up. Just don't let my sister give you too hard of a time."

"Which sister?"

"Both. I forgot to tell you that my whole family is coming. Expect it to be a loud dinner." She gave him a pained expression.

"I don't remember it being any other way," he said, smiling.

As they arrived at Lily's childhood home, Alex was suddenly overcome by memories of the years he'd spent walking up to this same door after school. Bill and Becky had been second parents to him, and standing on their front porch brought everything back.

Becky opened the door before they even knocked.

"Wow, Mom, that was fast. Were you waiting by the door?"

"The dog heard the truck when you pulled up. Oh, Alex, I'm so glad to see you." She opened her arms and gave him a big squeeze.

He had missed these kinds of family gatherings. Since his mom had moved away from Wild Harbor, he was lucky to see her once every few years. She had remarried five years ago, but her new husband had been anything but friendly toward Alex. He rarely received an invitation to their new home in Florida. It was almost like he had been pushed out of the family, an unpleasant reminder of his dad and all the memories from the past.

Which was why, after all this time, Lily's parents still felt like a second family. As he entered the familiar foyer, with its mauve and cream flowered wallpaper, the scent of fresh bread and baked pasta wafted through the home.

"It smells incredible."

"You were always a big eater in high school, so I expect you to have thirds."

"I'm not growing like I was back then, but I'm definitely hungry. Oh, these are for you." He handed her the bouquet.

"Flowers—my favorite. Thank you, Alex."

Becky disappeared into the kitchen to find a vase as they joined her dad in the living room.

Bill sat in his wheelchair, watching TV.

"Hey, Dad," Lily said, approaching him from behind.

He was slumped over slightly, but he sat up straighter when he heard his daughter's voice.

She bent over and kissed him. Alex noticed how frail Bill looked, but he still held a gentle smile for his daughter. He had always been a strong man, full of vitality, but now just a shadow of that fire flickered.

"Dad, do you remember Alex?"

Bill nodded. "Hi, Alex," he said in a slow but measured voice.

"Hey, Alex." Cassidy bounded into the room, followed by Megan and Matt.

"Wondered if you'd both come." Megan exchanged a look with Lily that he couldn't read. They still had a secret language Alex couldn't decipher.

Crowding around their dad to see the TV, Megan leaned over his shoulder. "What's the score now?"

"Tigers . . . by two," Matt said.

"Think they'll win?" Alex sat on the couch. "This hasn't exactly been their year so far."

"They can turn it around. Right, Dad?"

Bill nodded.

Matt gave Dad a pat on the shoulder. "If not, there's always next year."

Becky chirped from the kitchen, "The lasagna is ready." Matt pushed Bill's wheelchair to the dining room as Lily and the girls chatted about their day.

They sat around the table and Becky bowed her head to pray. "Lord, bless this meal, and thank you that Alex could join us. I pray we can be a blessing to him. Amen."

"So," Becky said, breaking the after-prayer silence. "Lily told us you're working on the house next to hers. How's that going?"

She dished out the first slice of lasagna for Alex. As she lifted it to his plate, melted cheese strung across the table like a trapeze wire.

"We're in the early stages at this point, but we haven't come across anything unexpected yet. It can throw a project off when we have unplanned repairs."

"Lily, maybe he should help you," Becky added, serving more lasagna.

"Actually, I have news." Lily's eyes brightened. "Alex proposed a double episode where they renovate two houses. He just got the green light from the production company that my house was chosen."

"What? That's wonderful news," Becky said as she passed the garlic bread to Alex.

Megan smiled at Lily, and a look passed between them.

The secret language again.

"I made him promise he'll let me help."

"As long as he keeps you from working too much," Becky said, cutting Bill's lasagna.

Cassidy grabbed a slice of bread and smiled. "Maybe Alex can help with that too."

Lily gave her sister a look of disapproval as she passed the salad to Alex and changed the subject. "Remember the window that's cracked over the door, Dad? I wonder if you know anyone who could repair it?"

Bill paused for a moment, searching for the words. Even though his speech was returning to normal since the stroke, he sometimes took long pauses before speaking. "Fix? Better off to replace." He paused once more, his eyes lighting up. "Joshua."

"Whose that?" Alex asked.

"He owns the salvage shop in town," Becky replied. "Not really open to the public, but he'll let you in because we go way back. He might have something from an old house that's been torn down. If he doesn't, he'll find it. I don't know where that man gets all his odds and ends, but he's a craftsman of a different kind."

"I can't believe that guy is even still alive. How old is he?" Matt scooped his last bite of lasagna.

Becky looked at her husband. "I don't know. Do you Bill?"

He shook his head.

"He was around when I was a little girl," Becky continued. "Been a fixture in this community ever since I can remember."

Matt passed his plate for a second helping of lasagna. "Cam told me a story about his grandfather. Joshua helped him fix his home after a thunderstorm knocked a huge tree limb into their roof. His grandfather tried to pay Joshua for his time, but he wouldn't take it. Just gave him some advice about how it was worth it to see his home look new again. He's a bit of mystery, from what I hear."

"Mystery is a good description." Becky put her fork down. "Joshua comes and goes as he pleases. He lives in a remote area outside town, then he disappears for a while. Folks don't know where he goes, but he always turns up right when he's needed."

Becky looked over at her husband, who was slumping in his seat, his eyelids drooping.

"The meal was good, but I'm . . . " Bill searched for the words.

"Tired?" Becky took her husband's hand. "I can save you a slice of pie for later. Why don't you rest? The kids and I can take care of things."

"I'll take Dad to the bedroom." Cassidy stood to push his wheelchair out of the dining room.

Becky headed into the kitchen to cut strawberry pie as Matt turned to Alex.

"You sure made Pammy's day." Matt held up his phone, revealing the selfie from the flower shop. "People are asking who received the flowers. Wait until they hear it's for Mom. Unless there's a secret girlfriend we don't know about."

Alex glanced at Lily and noticed her cheeks were flushed pink.

"Okay, who wants pie?" Becky came back, holding two plates of luscious strawberry pie topped with huge dollops of whipped cream. She set the plates in front of Alex and Lily before they could even respond.

"Becky, you've outdone yourself." Alex scooped a large strawberry covered in a cloud of white. "I haven't had homemade strawberry pie since I left Wild Harbor."

"Well, that's a crying shame. Everybody deserves homemade strawberry pie at least once a year, if not more." Becky laughed in that easygoing way that brought out the lines around her eyes.

Alex could see where Lily got her beauty.

Megan started gathering plates while Cassidy went to the kitchen to slice more pie.

"I'm going to skip pie." Megan pulled at the waistband of her jeans. "Looks amazing, but my pants are about to bust a button after Mom's lasagna."

"That never stopped me." Lily stuffed another bite in her mouth.

Megan picked up a spoon and pointed toward a door. "If I were eating dessert, I'd recommend enjoying it on the back porch. It's the perfect night for it." She gave Lily a quick wink and headed to the kitchen.

"Do you want to eat on the porch swing like old times?" Lily's smile took him back to high school. Unlocked memories.

She knew how to twist his arm with one look. She always had.

CHAPTER ELEVEN

ALEX

They stepped onto the back porch, the screen door squeaking shut the same way it had back in high school. So many things were identical to the picture in Alex's memory. The wooden porch swing. The giant maple in the middle of the yard. Becky's garden tucked back by the fence.

It was as if time had stopped, but they had moved on—for better or worse.

He sat on the porch swing, the one they had spent so much time on years ago, sharing their dreams for the future, wondering who they'd marry and how many kids they would have. "This brings back memories."

He started gently swinging as they ate their pie.

For all they had talked about marriage plans, it seemed ironic that neither of them were serious with anyone. Not that Alex hadn't had the chance. Usually, he'd found out the hard way that most of his dates were more interested in his fame than him. Lily saw him for who he was.

"Your mom's pie is the best."

"I told her she should start a bakery, and we could join forces. But you know Mom. She's committed to helping Dad. She never did get a chance to chase her dreams."

"Are you sure? Because I'd say her dreams were right here. You all mean the world to her."

"I guess it just seems so . . . normal, you know?"

"Normal life is underrated. I'd love to have what they have."

Lily paused. "Really? Because I thought you wanted the whole Hollywood thing. Fame. Fortune. The single life."

"Uh, no." He shook his head. "In this industry, nothing is as good as it looks."

"So go back to LA and find a nice girl, and then you'll be set." She licked the last bite of whipped cream off her plate. "A beautiful wife and a popular TV show. Everything you ever wanted."

Except it's not. "I'm not so sure about that," he replied, looking at her.

"What do you mean?"

"I *thought* that was the dream. Get a show, then settle down with a family. But life in LA is complicated. People climbing their way to the top. Friendships based solely on what you can get from someone. It can be ugly. What you have with your family is extraordinary, really."

"That's funny. I don't really think of it that way. Most days, I feel like a failure. My shop's struggling, and my luck with men has been—well, frankly, it's been a disaster. I thought it would be easy . . . it's been anything but." She pulled her feet on the swing and wrapped her arms around her legs, the same way she sat as a girl.

"I'll bet a bunch of guys would love to date you, they're just too scared to ask."

Lily burst out laughing. "I guess they don't realize I'd pretty much say yes to anyone right now. My calendar is wide open." She flung her arms out and leaned back into the swing.

"Okay, try me." Alex challenged her.

"What?" Lily sat up, a look of alarm on her face.

He leaned forward, locking eyes with her. "Would you say yes to me?"

She pulled back. "You can't ask me." She shook her head, her voice steady but determined.

"Why not?"

"You're feeling sorry for me. Just because I brought it up doesn't mean I'm a charity case."

Feeling sorry for you . . . hardly. "I didn't mean it that way."

"I don't believe you."

"Why not?"

"Why else would you have chosen my house for the second renovation? You want to help, but you don't have to offer to date me to make me feel better."

"Lily, that's not why I asked. Ever since I came back, I can't stop thinking of that moment in your house. Don't tell me you didn't feel it too."

She looked away, into the slowly darkening yard where the lightning bugs were beginning to emerge. "I think it would be best if we pretend that didn't happen."

Alex would have agreed with her before, but something had cracked open and shifted inside him. A longing that refused to stay dormant.

He turned to face her. "Do you remember what happened in this spot the night before graduation?"

"How could I forget?" she said avoiding his gaze. "I was mad at you all summer for trying to steal a kiss on the porch swing."

"I thought it was because you fell off trying to avoid me."

"That, too. I just couldn't believe you'd try to kiss me after going to prom with another girl. It was clear you didn't want an *actual* relationship, after pulling a stunt like that."

"How do you know?" he frowned.

"Because if you had, you would've asked me to the senior prom, instead of that bubblehead Priscilla."

Lily had retaliated by refusing to stay home and had asked Nathan Meyer to accompany her, just to spite Alex. When she had walked in, hanging on Nathan's arm, an off the shoulder, sparkly gown draping her perfect figure, Alex's mouth dropped open. *Serves you right.* She lifted her chin as she strolled by Alex.

Alex shifted on the swing, facing her. "At least Priscilla had a good reputation, unlike *your* date. Do you know how it felt to see you slow dancing with that creep?"

"You're calling my date a creep? I still remember the look of shock on your face when I showed up with Nathan. You interrupted us all night, cutting into our dances. Totally inappropriate."

Lily had no interest in dating Nathan, whose reputation as a flirtatious playboy repulsed her like the smell of a bad anchovy. But her choice was enough to enrage Alex, who had trailed Lily the rest of the night like a protective big brother, interrupting any time Nathan moved too close. She still relished the pathetic puppy dog look on Alex's face when she turned to leave, Nathan's arm wrapped around her bare shoulders.

Alex's eyes darkened. "I wanted to make sure he didn't touch you."

"So, you embarrassed me instead?"

"I wasn't trying to embarrass anyone. I wanted you to myself"

"And what do you want now?"

You.

It's what he wanted to say, but he shook his head, dodging her question. He still couldn't tell whether she had any intention toward him other than friendship. "I promised myself I wouldn't fall for anyone after Trina."

"The girl you dated in California?"

"Yes." He swallowed hard.

"Why? What happened?"

He hesitated, shifting in his seat. "Trina and I didn't break up. She passed away in an accident."

Lily took a deep breath. "I had heard that . . . I saw it on social media. I'm so sorry."

He shook his head, not wanting to talk about it again. But something in him wouldn't let him avoid this conversation. "That was my second loss, and it just confirmed what I knew—that love is a risk. I didn't ever want to open myself up to that kind of hurt again. But seeing your family—there's something in me that wants that kind of connection. Even though I drove you away in high school, I feel like you're the one person who might understand."

Lily looked away from him, out into the darkness of her backyard. "I don't know. I'm not the same girl I was back in high school. We're different people now." Flickering shadows danced in her distant expression.

"I don't want the high school you. I want to get to know the Lily right here." He touched her arm, his fingers gently sweeping down it.

This time, she didn't pull away.

"I don't understand what this means." He took her hand in his. "I'm afraid to even let myself try. But if you tell me tonight you have no interest in seeing where this leads, I won't bring it up again."

"Alex—" Her eyes searched the ground for something unseen, a grief she couldn't express. "After what's happened in my past with Thomas—"

Then she slowly brought up her face to look at him, sadness filling her eyes. "I can't."

She got up from the porch swing and left him in the dark, the screen door slamming shut.

CHAPTER TWELVE

LILY

Three days went by before she saw Alex again. He didn't try to contact her, and Lily resolved to keep her distance.

I won't think of Alex Briggs, she repeated to herself when she woke, hearing the pounding of hammers next door, while a drill whizzed in the background. It's not like he confessed anything more than an interest in her.

She looked out the window and spied the crew busy at work. Alex's gray truck was missing.

There was no way she would fall for a guy who spent his life on TV. He was everything she was not. Bold. Extroverted. Extremely handsome.

I bet he's around all kinds of beautiful women who love flirting with him.

She rubbed her forehead as if she could rub his memory right out of her mind. As she washed her face, she heard a knock at the door. Still in her pajama pants and tank top, she grabbed a cardigan and wrapped it around herself.

She asked through the door, "Who is it?"

"Uh, your personal food delivery service."

She opened the door a crack, enough to see that Alex had a box of something from The French Press Café. "You didn't tell me you were coming. I'm not even dressed." She tried to close the door.

He wedged it open with his foot.

"I'm not giving these to you unless you let me in." He put them behind his back.

"But I'm in my pajamas—"

He wouldn't remove his foot. "I'm here with a peace offering for the other night. So, you can either open the door and invite me in, or let your pride keep you from a delicious breakfast."

"Coffee cake?" She eyed the box.

"Close. Cinnamon rolls. Fresh this morning."

"Okay, you win." She opened the door. Enough for him to slide in without anyone seeing her.

He held the rolls and two cups of coffee.

"I accept your peace offering." She ran her hand through her messy hair. "Just don't make fun of me."

Alex sat on the kitchen counter, making himself at home. "I would never do that. But those are awfully cute pajamas."

She gave him a look and wrapped her cardigan around her even more.

He pulled out a roll covered in sweet icing. "You know it's demo day, right?"

"Uh, no. Was I supposed to prepare for that?" She squinted and looked off to the side, thinking hard. Her sisters had helped her pack up the living room and kitchen, but she still wasn't finished with her bedroom.

"No. Except you might want to get dressed because you'll be on camera."

"What? When?"

"Like in a few minutes."

"Seriously? How did I not know about this?"

"My assistant sent you an email with the details."

"Oh, no. I haven't checked my email for a few days. I've been busy planning the grand opening and packing my things. I need to go—" She stuffed a big chunk of roll in her mouth and ran into her bedroom. Then she stopped and poked her head around the doorframe. "Sorry to ask, but what am I supposed to wear?"

"You've never torn anything out of a house before? Wear old clothes."

"Not if I'm going to be on TV. And all my clothes are in boxes."

"Lily, you look good in anything. Even those pajamas."

"I'm not wearing pajamas," she said under her breath.

She closed the door and rested her forehead against it. *What have I done? I'm going to be on TV!*

The thought filled her with a mix of excitement and that dreaded feeling right before throwing up. She stuck her head out the door. "One more question—do I have to be on camera? You're the star. Why does anyone have to see me?" She wanted to beg, but she knew it was pointless.

"Because the boss asked. Don't worry, I'll do most of the talking. All you have do is stand there, look pretty, and swing a sledgehammer at that." He pointed to the dividing wall between the kitchen and living room. "Simple, right?"

"Right." She nodded and smiled. "Does it matter if I don't know how to swing a sledgehammer?"

"Not as long as you hit your target and not me." He gave her a mischievous grin.

She knew this was part of the agreement, but in her attempt to avoid him the last few days, she had neglected to even think about her role in the project. Or her wardrobe.

She was a mess. And now everyone in the country was going to know.

"You dress and I'll fetch the sledgehammer. We'll practice."

Lily shook her head as she took off her cardigan. Why had she agreed to this?

Because she was desperate. And broke.

She kicked a lone shoe across the floor and hit her broken closet door. Not that it mattered. Just one more thing on her long list of repairs. Without help, she'd never fix up this place. She sat on her bed and put her head in her hands. Alex's offer was the only option at this point.

When she came out wearing jeans and a T-shirt, Alex was holding a cinnamon roll in one hand and a sledgehammer in the other.

"Ready to practice?" He held up the tool like it was a prized weapon he was bestowing on her.

She reluctantly took it, feeling the weight.

"You want to hit the wall right in the middle with some muscle. Try a practice swing."

The tool felt heavy and unwieldy in her hands, so awkward compared to the kitchen tools she used for making chocolate. She lifted the sledgehammer and gave the wall a little tap.

Alex put his hand over his mouth and tried to hide his smile. "I know we're just practicing, but you're not going to get anywhere doing it that way."

"I'm just not cut out for this." She put the sledgehammer down.

"You can't hurt anything. We're destroying the wall. Take out all your stress on it. Like this." He took the tool and gave it a practice swing, then handed it back.

She took the sledgehammer, bent her knees, and stood like a baseball player ready for the first pitch.

Alex furrowed his brows. "Can I help you? Because your form looks kind of awkward."

"You said I couldn't do this wrong."

"Perhaps I was wrong." He was holding back a laugh but not doing a very good job.

It was enough to make her blood boil.

"At least I'm trying." She put her hands on her hips and frowned. "You're not helping . . ."

"I'm sorry, Lily." He covered his grin.

"Are you laughing at me?" She walked over to him with a death stare and the sledgehammer in the air.

He backed up and raised his hands, surrendering. "No! It's just—you looked like you were playing baseball. I know you wouldn't hurt a fly—"

"You wanna see me hurt something?" She turned to the wall. "I'll show you." With that, she swung the sledgehammer with a powerful thunk into the wall.

Alex sprang forward to stop her, but it was too late. Her blow socked an ugly gap in the wall, leaving the sledgehammer stuck in the hole.

Alex's mouth fell open. "Whoa! You were supposed to save that for when the cameras were here."

She took a step back, leaving the sledgehammer hanging mid-air. "Says who? It's my home. Now that I know how to swing this thing, I'm going to use it." She gave him a smile that challenged him to stop her.

He held out his hand and gave her his most charming smile. "Lily, I think I'll take that back before anything else happens."

"Nope." She returned the smile and grabbed the handle, pulling the bulky tool out of the wall. She held it in the air, and dared him to steal it from her.

"I need it." He said it calmly, like he was talking to a child.

She lifted her eyebrows, taunting him. "Then you'll have to chase it down first." She gave him a look that said *I dare you.* Then she turned and ran.

He chased after her as she escaped around a large packing box, but he cornered her next to a potted plant. She tried to dodge past him, but he grabbed her around the waist and hauled her over his shoulder, causing her to drop the hammer. She hung upside down as he laughed.

"Hey, no fair!" She kicked as she hung helplessly.

At that moment, the door squeaked open and a cameraman walked in. Lily was still upside down, the blood rushing to her face.

The cameraman looked at Alex then Lily. "Oh, sorry, am I interrupting something? Guess I should have knocked."

"Uh, no, come on in," Alex said, still holding Lily. "I just had to stop her from demolishing the wall before you arrived."

He set Lily on her feet with an apologetic smile as she gave him an unspoken, *I'll get you for this.*

Her heart still beat wildly from the chase—and how close they had been. Not that it was romantic to be thrown over a man's shoulder. If anything, it might have appeared a bit juvenile, but Lily had forgotten how much fun Alex could be and how much she had wanted, in that moment, to be touched by him.

She smoothed her shirt and hair, trying to look as if she hadn't been hanging like a monkey over Alex's shoulder.

More crew entered her home as Alex gave instructions and checked some last-minute script changes.

As she sat down at the table and rested her chin on her hand, Lily observed how Alex took control. With his muscular shoulders and piercing blue eyes, she couldn't help but admire his good features. *And goodness knows, he had plenty of them.*

This was not the Alex she remembered from high school. He was someone people looked up to and respected. Successful. Gorgeous.

Who was she to think he would fall for her?

He caught her staring and gave her a quick smile that nobody else saw.

A shot of energy pulsated through her. She was still the same foolish girl who had been willing to fall for a guy way above her league. But this time, she couldn't let herself dream about the future. Life had been too cruel to believe she could trust someone again.

Alex came over and bent down next to her. "Are you nervous?"

She nodded.

He put his hand on her arm. "You shouldn't be. You'll be amazing at this. What could possibly go wrong?"

Everything.

WHEN IT WAS time to record, Alex stepped in front of the lights and took control, explaining the project with his natural charm. He appeared so calm and self-assured, while Lily stood awkwardly behind him, trying not to let her hands shake. All she had to do was join him on camera for demolishing the wall, and he'd take care of the rest.

"You're up," one of the crew whispered to her.

Her heart was hammering in her chest.

Alex waved her over and gave her a reassuring smile while handing her a sledgehammer. "You ready for this?"

"As ready as I'll ever be." Her mouth went dry as she picked up the heavy tool.

"Okay, on the count of three, let's smash this wall. One, two, three!"

Lily swung the sledgehammer and it sliced into the wall with a neat thud, making a nice hole in the exterior. Again and again, they took turns smashing holes until Lily started giggling. "I never thought I'd say it, but this is fun. Maybe even therapeutic."

"I told you it would be."

When they finished recording, Alex turned to Lily. "I had no idea you loved destroying things so much."

Still elated from demolishing the wall, she grinned at him. "Me neither. I'm not sure what that says about me."

"To be honest, it's one of my favorite parts, a total stress reliever. It's that moment when you know you can't go back. As soon as you destroy something, you've made your decision to move forward."

Kind of like life, she wanted to say.

"Hey, I noticed the window you were talking about to your dad—the one over the door. We can look for a replacement for you."

"I know, but it's the original window. I don't want to lose it." Lily walked to the window. The crack did look pretty bad.

"It is a beauty, but it's not in good shape."

She sighed. "What if we found a window at a salvage shop?"

Alex shook his head. "I doubt we'd be able to find a good one that will fit. It's like a needle in a haystack."

"What about the man my dad was talking about—Joshua? We might be able to find it at his place."

Alex shrugged.

Lily knew it was a long shot, but she didn't want to give up just yet. "Why don't we head over and see?" She hoped, this time, she would get her way. "You need to meet Joshua anyway. He's the type of guy you don't forget."

CHAPTER THIRTEEN

LILY

When they arrived at Joshua's shop, the sky threatened rain, dark clouds rolling in as they found the doors to his store locked. Calling it a store was probably too generous a term.

"It doesn't look like much in there," Alex said, peering through a window. "It looks like all the castaways and trash no one wants."

"I haven't been here since I was a little girl, but I remember it as the most fascinating place, filled with all kinds of treasures if you just took the time to look."

"Well, it's not been kept up very well. Looks like stuff most people would throw out."

"I guess we're not most people. My dad has found several things here, but his visits with Joshua are the real treasure. You'd never guess it—he's a quiet man, full of wisdom."

"Maybe full of wisdom, but not in a business sense. I'm not sure how this guy stays in business. He has just as many broken things as your home does." He gave her a smile.

"Gee, thanks. But unlike me, fixing broken things is his specialty." Drops started to sprinkle from the ominous clouds, peppering them. "Have you tried knocking?" Lily walked to the door and pounded on it.

"Doesn't look like anyone is there," Alex said. "I suppose he doesn't need to keep any hours. Not like he has a lot of customers."

The bolt clicked, and the door slowly opened. An old man stood on the other side, holding a screwdriver and an antique light fixture he had been working on. His face was weathered and wrinkled, but his smile held a warmth.

"I wondered when you would come," he said looking at them both. "Sorry to keep you waiting. Come inside before the storm hits."

Alex glanced at Lily before she stepped through the door into the shop.

The old man walked ahead, his body surprisingly agile and his eyes sharp. Lily found strange comfort being in his presence, as if he were an old friend. She looked around at his vast collection, the piles of old doors and windows, heavy wood mantels and antique light fixtures. The shelves of odds and ends, rescued from demolished homes and renovation projects. Unusual metal door latches and cut glass doorknobs, intricate metal hooks, and ornate vent covers. He saw value in hodgepodge that looked like junk, trinkets from years gone by.

"What can I do for you, Lily?"

"You remember me?" She stared at him, trying to find out how he knew who she was. It's not like she had come in recently. The last time she could remember was when she was ten. His face was tanned, and his eyes contained a warmth that drew her into his presence. He was tall, but not imposing, and though he moved with an unhurried gait, his body was agile, his fingers nimble. His laughter was like waterfalls, refreshing and full.

"Oh, yes. You've grown up since you last were here. But I see your father regularly. He can't stop telling me how proud of you he is."

Her dad wasn't one to lavish compliments on his kids, so she never dreamed he would tell Joshua.

Lily looked down at the old floorboards in the shop, etched with age. How many people had walked through here with the hopes of finding something they needed?

"I don't know why he would say that." She didn't want Joshua to know how she really felt about the turn of events in her life, especially since failure seemed to be a regular occurrence. If anything, most people would say she had nothing to show for the last eight years.

Nothing. The pain of that word hit her in the stomach.

Joshua turned suddenly and put his hand on Alex's shoulder. "Alex, welcome back to town."

Alex frowned slightly when Joshua addressed him. "Thanks, but I don't remember ever meeting you when I lived here."

Joshua smiled, looked down at the light fixture in his hand, and placed it on a table nearby. It was an antique sconce that held one small bulb.

"We didn't meet, exactly. But I knew your parents. They came by often."

Alex paused, taking in Joshua's words. "I didn't know that. They never talked about you."

"They told me a lot about you. That's how parents are. Always worried about their kids, no matter how old they get. It's a sign of love, really."

"So, you know about my father?"

Joshua nodded slowly. "I know his death broke your mother's heart. She struggled with understanding why."

Alex looked away.

Lily couldn't read his expression, but she sensed he didn't want to talk about it.

"How is she these days?" Joshua asked. "Haven't seen her in some time."

"She moved to Florida and remarried. With my travel schedule, I don't see her much. To be honest, her second husband hasn't exactly been welcoming. I remind him too much of my dad, and that creates some issues. It's like he wants to forget Mom ever had a life before they married."

Something flashed through Alex's eyes as he said it, an unspoken hurt behind the words. He hid it well, but Joshua had uncovered just enough for Alex to reveal the old wound again.

"I see." Joshua spoke slowly as he rubbed a cloth across the light fixture, delicately cleaning it. "So, what can I help you folks find?"

"I have a window in my home that's cracked," Lily said. "Alex wants to replace it with a new one. I wanted to come here and see if you have anything similar."

"Similar? No. But something unexpected that might take some work? Possibly," Joshua said with a small grin.

Alex shook his head. "I told her I had my doubts we would find anything."

Joshua nodded slowly and looked from Alex to Lily. "He might be right."

"But what about fixing it?" Lily asked. "My dad said you can fix anything."

"Your dad is a generous man. But sometimes broken things . . . need more than that."

Lily's smile faded. She could feel Alex's eyes on her, but she refused to look at him. She couldn't bear his silent message of *I told you so*.

"Can I see the measurements?" Joshua asked.

Alex pulled a paper from his pocket and handed it to the old man.

He scanned the paper. "It *might* work. With some adjustments. Follow me to the back." Joshua ambled away, leaving the light fixture on the table.

They weaved through a series of small rooms, stacked with parts from bygone homes. Floor to ceiling bookshelves. Ornate crown molding and dark paneled doors. Beautiful remnants of grand homes, now torn down. These fragments were the only things remaining of family histories.

Lily listened to the rain pounding on the roof now. Did history always have to be a reminder of how fragile life was?

"The windows are back here." Joshua pointed to an area ahead. "Most windows don't make it to my shop. The few that do are special. They're the strong that survive everything life throws at them."

Joshua began to sift through the stacked windows resting against the wall.

Alex focused on another stack, moving past Joshua to see more of the windows he had collected. "I don't see anything that looks even close. It's a long rectangular shape."

"I'm looking for one I've had for ages. The perfect one."

Lily peered over Joshua's shoulder as he filtered through the stack. She glanced at Alex, who shook his head discreetly.

"Here it is." Joshua pulled out a window neatly tucked away in an old blanket. "Wrapped up for safekeeping."

He laid it on the floor and carefully unwrapped the blanket while Lily kneeled to inspect it more closely.

As he uncovered the last part, she traced her finger across the brilliant hues of stained glass. Through a thick layer of dust and dirt, the rich purples and deep reds vividly stood out in the dim light. In the middle, the glass formed a picture, but she couldn't decipher it.

"It's beautiful," she gasped. "But what is it?"

"The picture will become clearer once I clean it and do some repair work. But look in the bottom corner." With his finger, he wiped away a smudge of dirt and dust, uncovering a white flower in each corner. "Do you recognize this?"

"A white lily," she said.

"The owners grew them along the west end of their property."

"How long have you had this?" Alex inspected it more closely.

Joshua shook his head. "Long time. It came out of the Riner home on Market Street, which caught fire at the turn of the century. The fire was put out before it could destroy everything, but the home was too damaged to restore. Luckily, this window was rescued from the demolition and has been waiting for its new owner ever since."

He nodded toward Lily.

"It's extraordinary. But will it work?" She looked at Alex.

He had already pulled out his measuring tape and was shaking his head. "It's close and would take some work. I'm not sure if we can fit it in with everything else that needs to be done."

Joshua nodded. "I'll work on cleaning it up. You know where to find me if you want it." He stood and walked away silently, his work with them done.

Lily picked up the window slowly, afraid of breaking such an extraordinary piece. "You couldn't find a beauty like this anywhere. Do you think it's possible we could make it work?"

Alex took the window from her, shaking his head. "I don't know, but I'll see what I can do. Just don't get your hopes up yet."

She squealed and wrapped her arms around his waist, causing Alex to nearly lose his balance.

He laughed. "You're going to make me drop this window, and then we'll be in real trouble."

His gaze dropped to her lips, like he was going to lean in and kiss her.

Her heart skipped. She let go of him and took a step back.

"I need to head into the shop for the afternoon. We probably should head back."

He nodded, the moment gone.

As they walked through the salvage shop, they tried to find Joshua to express their thanks, but he was nowhere to be seen.

CHAPTER FOURTEEN

LILY

Alex rattled her. Made her jumpy. Lily threw another shirt into her suitcase.

"Cass, I thought you came over to help me." She tossed a T-shirt toward her sister.

Cassidy lounged across the bed, scrolling on her phone, ignoring the clothing that landed next to her elbow. Her youngest sister had stopped by to pack the last of her clothing and pick up the cat.

"Oh, my goodness, you won't believe it!" Cassidy sat up and turned her phone so Lily could read it.

Someone from the crew had taken a shot of Lily smashing a hole in her wall and posted it online. Somehow the mayor's office had reposted it, and now it had gone viral with a stream of comments and predictions about whether she and Alex were dating.

Lily rolled her eyes. "Looks like gossip for the rumor mill." Lily folded a pair of shorts and placed it in her suitcase, replaying that moment with Alex.

Cassidy started organizing Lily's suitcase. "So, what is going on with you two? I see that little smirk on your face."

"What do you mean? This is how I always look."

Cassidy glared at her sister. "Not since everything happened with Thomas. I know things have been hard the last few months. Alex seems to be good for you."

"He's just a friend, if that's what you're asking."

"I'm not implying anything. I just wondered if anything happened between you two."

"Not beyond him helping me get this house in shape." Lily thought of their moment at Joshua's when Alex had looked like he was going to kiss her. The heat prickled on her neck. "We are heading out tonight for dinner. But it's *not* a date."

"Just you two? I call that a date." Cassidy plopped onto the bed next to Lily's suitcase, smiling.

"It's not. He just hates eating alone."

"Mm-hmm. Right." Her sister nodded like she didn't believe her.

"Don't tell Mom. Or Megan. Definitely not Matt. I'll never hear the end of it."

"I won't tell—as long as you spill the dirt later."

"There won't be any dirt," Lily said, putting her hands on her hips.

Her sister giggled as she fell back on the bed. "I can't believe you're going out with Alex Briggs!"

Lily picked up her pillow and hit her sister on the arm. "You're not helping me feel better."

She wondered whether she had made the right decision to go out with Alex since already her sister was making assumptions. It was enough to make her want to cancel their plans, splurge on takeout, and watch a sappy movie that made her cry.

"Don't say a word," Lily warned her sister. "If you do, I'm not going."

"Don't worry. Your secret's safe with me."

As seven o'clock approached, Lily donned a blue dress with sandals and grabbed a jacket just in case the evening turned chilly. The afternoon had been wonderfully balmy, and the May flowers were exploding with color. The sun was setting over the lake, drenching everything in gold. Lily stepped onto her porch and sat down in an Adirondack chair to watch the waves roll in.

She would miss this view while she stayed with her parents. How many times had she sat in this chair and prayed for God to bring an end to her struggles?

Mesmerized by the waves, she heard footsteps come around the side of the house.

"There you are," Alex said. He was dressed in a white short-sleeved shirt and a pair of khaki shorts.

Did he ever not look like a million bucks?

He grinned. "I knocked. When no one answered, I thought you had bailed on me."

How could I, with that smile? Her heart melted just a little. "I was just out here enjoying the view one last time."

"Not your last time. The view will be even better when you move back."

When you're gone. She wouldn't think about his goodbye, at least, not tonight. She had spent her whole life anticipating the bad things that might happen. For once, she just wanted to enjoy a night out. "Why won't you tell me where we're headed? You're not going to take me on an outdoor adventure where a dress would be a terrible idea, right?"

"Not at all. You look beautiful."

Her cheeks began to burn. "Uh, thanks." She stood quickly, hoping he wouldn't notice the heat rising in her face.

"By the way, I should warn you that a picture leaked to social media."

"I already heard. Cassidy couldn't wait to tell me."

"Yeah, sorry. That wasn't supposed to happen. That's why I changed our plans. I didn't want to eat at a restaurant where you'd feel . . . "

"On display?"

"Exactly. I already picked up tapas from Lolita's. I thought we could eat on the beach tonight." He motioned to the stretch of white sand past the white gate. "You're not tired of the water, right?"

Lily turned toward the beach. "I could never tire of this. But I can't believe you ordered tapas."

He cut her off. "I know I didn't *have to*, but I wanted to. In high school, I used to dream about going to that place, but I could never afford it."

"I would have been fine with a burger."

"I'm not going to take you to a fast-food restaurant. You deserve better."

Alex picked up the carryout boxes from his truck while Lily grabbed a beach blanket and headed through the white gate that led to the beach. The stretch of creamy sand was gloriously empty. Too often, she didn't have time to cross that magical entry point onto the beach. Walking through the gate was like an invitation to escape all her problems, beckoning her to slow down. She took a deep breath and sensed Alex's presence behind her.

She turned suddenly and noticed he was staring at her. "What is it?" She asked, embarrassed she'd been caught totally unawares.

"You standing there, looking so happy, for a moment I thought . . ."

"What?"

"I was back in high school. You brought back a distinct memory of when we went to the beach and talked so late that our parents were mad at us."

"How could I forget? You dared me to go into the water in

my clothes. And I was stupid enough to do it." She laughed as they walked through the sand. "I don't get out here enough. But when I do, I sit and watch the sailboats on the water." She spread the blanket on the sand and sat.

"If I lived in Wild Harbor, I'd be here as much as possible." He unpacked the food and handed her a box. "It's not like being at a restaurant, but I hope this is just as memorable. By the way, I hope you're not sick of chocolate."

"Oh, no, I could never be sick of chocolate." She opened the basket she kept stocked for a picnic and started plating the food. "Why don't you have a dozen girls asking you out?"

"I don't want to."

"So, you *do* have a dozen girls?"

"Unless I know them, the answer is no. Most just want the spotlight. You can tell with one conversation that they're more interested in falling for the guy on TV than in getting to know who I actually am." He paused and looked at the waves. "That's why Trina was different. After her death, I just couldn't seem to move on." He pushed the food around with his fork.

"She must have been really special."

"She was." Alex put his plate down. "It's not easy to talk about, but I was driving when the accident happened. Just crossing the intersection when a guy ran a red light. T-boned the passenger side where Trina was riding. I blamed myself—if I had only been paying more attention, everything would have been different."

"It wasn't your fault." Lily reached out and touched his arm. "You know that, right? That accident was not your fault."

"I know. But I have these moments when I can't stand the guilt. She hadn't wanted to leave her apartment, and I pushed her to go." He shook his head and looked down at his hands. "Every time I hear an ambulance, my heart jumps out of my chest. I'm not sure how to move on after what happened. I made a promise I wouldn't fall for anyone. I'm just not sure I can take the risk."

Lily's hand was still on his forearm as she rubbed her thumb across his skin.

He paused, then lifted his eyes to meet hers. "What about you? Why aren't you dating someone?"

"To be honest, I haven't really wanted to date since Thomas."

"What happened?"

A few seagulls landed on the sand nearby, eyeing their food. Images flashed through her mind.

Thomas grabbing her arm, the pressure of his fingers pinching her skin.

"You're hurting me," she had told him, before he'd let go.

He had been upset with her—she couldn't even remember why—and his anger had boiled over for a second.

She took a deep breath. "I thought it was a one-time thing. He seemed like such a nice guy in the beginning. The perfect gentleman. Then, one day, he got angry about something really small. I had forgotten something he had left at my place. He grabbed my wrist and said, 'Don't do it again.'"

The sting of shame pierced her. "I thought it was my fault he was so angry because I had messed up. But then it happened again. A little shove here. A push there. I was working so hard to please him. I believed it was *my* problem. One day, he pushed too hard, and I lost my balance and fell. I realized I had to get out of there before something worse happened.

"I ended up at Megan's, where I confessed what was happening. She told me, 'A man who loves you wouldn't make you feel threatened.' I wondered how I had gotten to that place." Her voice choked as she blinked back tears. "I never thought I would date someone so dangerous and not know it."

He took her arm and pulled her close. "Lil, I'm so sorry. No man should ever treat a woman that way."

Lily nodded as her head rested against his chest. "I know

that now. But back then, I thought it was my fault. That was the strange part. Thomas *seemed* nice. But he had this other side that lashed out when he was angry. After I broke things off, I started to question whether I could really choose a nice guy who would treat me right, the way my father treats me. It's just easier to avoid dating altogether." Lily pulled away from Alex.

His eyes searched hers, revealing a sadness she hadn't seen before. "Lily, if I had known any of this, I wouldn't have asked you out tonight. I don't want you to feel—"

She stopped him, placing her hand on his. "No, don't feel bad. I *know* you. You're not like Thomas at all."

"I'd never hurt you, and I'd never let anyone else hurt you either."

She paused. "I know."

"But I was wondering . . . if I can help you move on from your past and trust again?"

"But how?" She looked at him.

"What if I helped you feel safe?"

"Alex—" She had confessed the damage Thomas had done to her heart, but she was still wounded. If he had expectations that she could just get over it and move on, she had to set him straight.

"Hear me out," Alex said, determination in his eyes. "Let me show you how a woman should be treated. Starting tonight."

She began to say something, then stopped. He was right. Even if her heart felt conflicted about him, she wasn't committing to anything beyond this evening. She could at least say yes to that.

AFTER THEY ATE DESSERT, the sunset hovered over the water, turning everything to rich orange and brilliant rose reds.

Lily took off her shoes to bury her toes in the sand. The

glow drenched everything in color, and Lily couldn't remember the last time she'd spent so much time watching the sunset or walking the beach. The last six months had been, to put it mildly, exhausting. She usually scarfed down dinner and fell into bed each night after spending the day working nonstop. Some days, Lily felt like her body was running on fumes.

This moment with Alex was exactly what her body needed. A long dinner. Conversation. Sand between her toes.

He stood and held his hand out for her.

"I'm not sure I can stand up after that dinner." She flopped backward on the blanket.

Instead of pulling her up by the hand, he bent over and scooped her up off the ground.

"What are you doing?"

"What does it look like?"

"I'm perfectly capable of walking."

"Perfect and capable. Yes." He caught her gaze for a moment as he held her, feet dangling off the ground. Then he put her down gently.

She wished he hadn't let go.

They walked into the waves, the chilly water splashing over their feet. There was only silence between them until Lily brought up what had been on her mind more than once since Alex had returned.

"Have you thought about your dad since coming home?"

"Yes, so much here reminds me of him. Every storefront and street corner. Even the beach. It's like I keep seeing him even though I know he's not here. But the strange thing is, I don't mind anymore." He peered down the beach. "When I left Wild Harbor, I was trying to run away from my memories. I was a wreck."

Lily hooked her arm through his.

"Then, after Trina died, I was mad that my worst fears— losing someone I loved—had happened not once, but twice. I wrestled with the question—if God could have stopped this, why didn't He?"

Lily leaned into him more. "My mom always reminds me that God is good, and He is safe; it's just the world that's not."

"I know that in my head. I just wish it was easier to believe."

"Me too. It's not that I doubt God's goodness or His plan. I just wonder how painful it will be."

He stopped and turned to her. "Do you know one reason why I like talking with you?"

She shook her head.

"Because you don't judge me for telling you things I'm afraid to say to anyone else." He took her hands and looked at her for a moment.

Lily had a sudden realization that the conversation had turned into something more than confessing their deepest wounds.

Longing filled his eyes as he leaned forward and gently brushed her lips with his.

For once, she didn't feel the weight of panic pressing on her chest or the memory of Thomas's anger flashing before her.

For so long, she had carried shame. It had become an ugly, festering wound that would not allow her to open her heart, no matter how hard she tried.

She closed her eyes and let Alex's tender kiss begin to heal the scars of her past. She knew he would not hurt her, not the way others had.

He pulled his lips away, but continued to hold her as she rested her head on his shoulder.

She understood what it meant to be free and healed and loved. If only for now.

CHAPTER FIFTEEN

ALEX

"Where does this leave us?" he asked at the end of the night as they walked the beach.

"Us?"

"Yeah, us." He stopped, waiting for her answer.

"Alex, tonight was wonderful."

He looked at her, and for once, he didn't see the fear behind her eyes.

"But you and I both know this would never work."

He started to interrupt, but she shook her head and put her hand on his chest. "Please don't try to talk me out of it. If things were different . . ." She hesitated. "But we can't change the choices we've made."

He wanted to argue. To prove to her that no matter what had happened in their past, they could make things work now. But he knew debating with Lily was not the way to win her heart. If he was going to convince her, he had to take it slow. Lily always had been his first love, the one his soul had been searching for.

Tonight had chiseled away something deeper between them, but he knew what she needed most was more time.

It was the one thing he didn't have.

Even if he went back to Phil and begged for an extension, what could that give him? A week, if that?

No matter how he tried to rearrange his schedule, he couldn't figure out how to extend his time in Wild Harbor. If he was honest with himself, he wondered if Lily actually might be right.

~

DURING THE NEXT FEW DAYS, the renovation on the house ramped up, leaving Alex with little time to see Lily.

He didn't want her to think he was avoiding her after their conversation, so he sent her a quick message.

Alex: Loved our dinner on the beach and can't wait to see you again. Need to get some work done on the house next door for the next few days.
Lily: I understand, but don't forget about me.

Like that was even possible.

If he could turn back time, he wouldn't have left Wild Harbor when he was twenty-two. He would have waited for her to graduate from college.

Alex shook the thought away. He couldn't change the past or who he was now.

"A work in progress," his therapist had told him.

Maybe that's why he liked renovating these fixer-uppers. He could tear up the past and rebuild it from scratch. All the damage, ripped out and destroyed.

If only that worked on humans.

As he looked at the house, he felt a tap on his shoulder.

"Hey, Alex. I finally made it to Wild Harbor."

He turned to see Alli, the beautiful and slightly bossy interior designer who joined him on his home show.

"Alli, I thought you weren't coming in until tomorrow."

"You know how I am. Couldn't stay away." She gave him a flirty smile.

Alex shifted his eyes from her raven hair toward Lily's house, trying to avoid her gaze.

"This town is cute, but a bit small for my taste. I mean if you blinked, you'd miss it. Where on earth am I going to get my materials for these houses?"

"I'm sure you'll find a way." He gave her a tight-lipped smile.

"I'll have to ship everything overnight. By the way, I didn't eat breakfast. Do you want to head to that coffee shop in town and discuss the project?"

Alex was less than thrilled about spending time alone with Alli, but they needed to nail down details for the design. A born and bred LA girl, she was everything Lily was not—dripping with strong perfume and high-end bags, expensive designer heels, and leather jackets. Alli embodied the philosophy of "more is more," upgrading not only her looks, but also her love life. She always looked for the next best thing, whether it was purses or men.

As they walked toward the truck, he noticed Lily's car was now parked in her drive. Alli was the last person he wanted to introduce to Lily. If she sensed any chemistry between him and Lily, she'd have it all over the Internet in hours, if only to spite him for not dating her. Alex took one look at Lily's house, then opened the door to his truck.

~

THE FRENCH PRESS Café was busy all morning, but they'd just hit a lull when Alex and Alli entered.

109

He scanned the room, breathing in the aroma of freshly brewed coffee.

In the corner, a few ladies chatted around a table, discussing the same book. A couple of college students huddled at a table in the back while two moms, flanked by strollers, held sleeping babies. A lone businessman sat at a table talking on his cell phone.

When Alex walked in, the book club ladies did a double take. One lady, with hair like a cloud of white, leaned over to her friend. "That's the TV star!"

Another woman from the book club walked over to him, her eyes bright. "Alex Briggs! I remember when you were just a boy at Wild Harbor Elementary. My, you've grown up!" Her smile was like warm cocoa on a winter's night. "I'm Diane Sutton. You went to school with my daughter, Mila."

He could place Mila's face in his head, but hadn't seen her since graduation. "Yes, I remember her. What is she up to these days?"

"Owns a bridal shop in Chicago. So, if you know anyone getting married . . ." She raised her eyebrows, hinting.

"I don't, actually." He wasn't about to tell Diane that he had no intentions of tying the knot.

Diane squeezed his arm like his grandma used to. "We're excited to have you back. How long are you staying?"

"About six weeks." Alex heard Alli clear her throat, a signal she was done with this conversation. "By the way, this is the interior designer who works on the show, Alli."

Alli nodded toward Diane with a tight smile. Her eyes flitted back to the good-looking barista making an espresso.

Alex tried to elbow Alli, but she didn't notice. It was one of the reasons Alex had no interest, despite her numerous attempts to ask him out. Underneath, she wasn't looking for a long-term commitment, only another step in her career.

"Well, Diane, so nice to see you again," Alex said. "Tell Mila hello from me."

"Oh, where are my manners? Let me introduce you to Max, the owner of this coffee shop. He's new to Wild Harbor."

They walked to the counter where Diane gave Max the same warm smile. "Max, I want to introduce you to Alex Briggs. He grew up here and went to school with my daughter Mila."

Max extended his hand toward Alex in a firm handshake. "Welcome back to Wild Harbor."

Alli took a step forward toward Max and gave him her most seductive smile. "I'm Alli Castleton, interior designer for the show."

Max nodded at Alli, but seemed unaffected by her charms.

Good man.

Diane added, "You must try one of the scones, they're a specialty."

Alli rolled her eyes. "I can't eat scones. I'm gluten-free. Besides, those things are horribly fattening—"

Alex quickly cut Alli off. "I'll take one and a latte. Don't skimp on the cream."

Alli gave him a dirty look.

He loved rubbing it in that he didn't care what he ate, which aggravated Alli, who was on a gluten-free vegan paleo diet and probably a few other things Alex couldn't remember, which annoyed her even more. She was one of those staunch always-on-a-new-diet types, the kind of person who lists their restrictions with something akin to religious fervor, and not because she actually couldn't eat those things, but because it was the hot trend. Alex wasn't even sure what she was allowed to eat. She seemed to exist on air.

"I'll take a water with a slice of lemon," Alli added.

"Well, it was nice to see you both." Diane tapped his arm. "Alex, if you're ever in need of a home-cooked meal, we'd love to have you over for dinner."

"I might just take you up on that." He smiled at Diane before she walked back to her table.

He leaned over to Alli and whispered, "You could at least pretend to be friendly."

She gave him an impatient sigh. "Why? I'm not going to see these people ever again." She looked at the handsome barista. "Except for him."

Alex got the sense she was trying to make him jealous. Truthfully, he was relieved to be rid of her attention.

She leaned on the counter, resting her head on her hand, trying to catch Max's eye. "What's there to do for fun? I mean, other than get coffee."

The barista glanced briefly her way then focused on his espresso. "It's finally warm enough to hang out at the beach, although the water is still chilly. Doesn't stop me, though."

"You're crazy. I am definitely not getting in cold water. Well, unless, I could warm up in a hot tub afterward."

Max didn't even look at her, thwarting her efforts to bait him with her flirting.

"Latte and a scone for Alex." He handed Alex his drink and whispered, "Good luck with your project—and her." He nodded toward Alli while she checked her phone.

A look of understanding passed between the men.

"And one water with lemon."

Alli gave him a smile. "If you ever need to look me up, the name is Alli Castleton."

Max nodded then looked at Alex.

He felt bad for the guy. "We'll be sure to recommend this place to our crew. Thanks, Max."

Alli sat at a table as Alex bit into a buttery scone. She furrowed her brow. "I thought you were eating healthy now."

"I thought you weren't coming until tomorrow."

He took another big bite.

"Sounds like you didn't like my little surprise. I thought you could show me around town today."

Alex opened his arms wide. "Welcome to Wild Harbor. You've already seen it all on our five-minute drive here."

"Funny. I meant you could show me your high school haunts. The places you hung out. Where you took girls on dates. That sort of thing." She smiled.

Alex noticed her red-lined lips needed a touch-up. He bristled in his seat. "I've got work to do."

"I even floated the idea past our boss. I said we should include clips of you coming back to your roots—the hometown boy who made good. He liked the idea."

Alex could only imagine what the guys from high school would say about that. "I don't want the focus on me, and my friends aren't looking for TV exposure. Plus, I've got a lot of work to do. In case you haven't heard, we're doing two houses."

"Oh, yes, the dump next door. Don't these people know how to take care of their houses?"

Alex swallowed hard, trying not to be enraged by Alli's quick judgment of Lily's home. "There's a reason. The family has been through some tough things in the last six months. We're going to help them out, turn things around for them. It might help to have some compassion."

She cocked her head to the side and widened her eyes. "I have compassion. I'm just not a bleeding heart like you, Alex."

Before he could respond, his phone buzzed in his pocket, interrupting his line of thought. "Hello?"

"Hey, Alex, it's Matt. Lily took a fall at her place, and she's hurt her ankle pretty bad."

"What happened?"

"Well, she didn't want me to tell you, but she tripped. I need someone to be on call for her. I'm heading to work, but I told her she shouldn't put any weight on it. Will you be around in case she needs someone? Cass and Megan went out of town today, and I hate to ask Mom since she's taking care of Dad."

"Of course, no problem. In fact, I'll swing by right now and see how she is."

"Yeah, just don't tell her I told you. She's going to have a fit because . . . you know how she is . . . always refusing help because she wants to do things on her own."

"Yeah, sounds familiar. I'll be right over."

He ended the call and looked at Alli. "An emergency came up. I can't talk through details right now. We'll catch up later."

"Right now?"

"Yes. You coming or staying?"

Alli looked at the barista again, who continued to avoid her gaze. "I guess I'm coming." She slowly stood as Alex walked over to Max.

"Can I get one more scone to go? For a friend."

"Sure thing, man. It's on the house." He dropped the scone into a bag and handed it to him.

"Thanks." Alex walked out of the coffee shop with Alli trailing after, her high-heeled mules clicking across the floor.

"But Alex, who am I supposed to hang out with today?"

Her whiny voice and clicking heels grated on Alex's last nerve. He swung around to face her. "I'm not your cruise director, Alli. I'm sure you can find something useful to do."

Her mouth dropped open as he walked toward his truck in silence.

There was only one person on his mind now.

CHAPTER SIXTEEN

LILY

"I'm not staying on this couch all day. I've got to get ready for the grand opening. It's in less than two weeks." Lily put her foot on the floor to test her pain level.

Matt stood over his sister. "Either you rest your ankle, Lily, or you head to the doctor's office. Your choice."

She scowled and crossed her arms. She hated ultimatums. "I'm not going to the doctor's office just for a sprain. That'll cost me even more money I don't have."

"Then I'm glad your couch didn't get moved yet. Otherwise, you'd be sitting on the floor."

She couldn't believe this was happening *now*, when she most needed to be on her feet working. She had stupidly tripped over the threshold of her front door when she'd come into the house, distracted by Alex talking with that beautiful dark-haired lady with the red lipstick. She hadn't been paying attention as she'd raced into the house to find some chocolate molds and turned her ankle.

Not only was she a klutz, but a jealous klutz. Now she was paying the price.

The front door swung open as Alex entered her living room, concern on his face.

Speak of the devil.

"Alex, what are you doing here?"

"I heard the news and came from my meeting."

"Who told you?" She looked from Alex to her brother, and her mouth fell open. "Matt, did you tell him?"

Alex stifled a smile as she glared at Matt.

Her brother shrugged. "I'm heading to the fire station now. You two have fun." He bolted to the door, slamming it behind him.

"That answers my question. But next time, you should really knock."

"I didn't want you to come to the door when you should stay off your ankle. Let me see it."

"I'm fine. I'm sure Matt made way too big of a deal about it."

Alex picked up her foot like he was cradling a baby chick. "Why didn't you call me?"

Because of her.

She winced as he took off the ice pack and examined the swelling. Her ankle looked like it was growing a ping-pong ball under the skin. "Matt sees hurt people all the time. It's cheaper than a doctor."

"Matt's a firefighter, not a doctor. You should really get an X-ray."

"No, thanks. I have enough bills to worry about. I'm just going to ice it and see how it goes."

"If it still looks bad tomorrow, I'm paying for a doctor's exam." He handed her a bag. "Maybe this will help."

She peeked inside. "You shouldn't have."

She took a bite of the scone and closed her eyes, enjoying the butter-laden treat. *How did Alex know that food is the way to my heart?*

She wished he'd bring her something terrible, like a piece of old gum. "I still can't let you help me. What about the house next door?"

"That's what my crew is for. I'll step in to film as needed. Besides, my interior designer loves the spotlight. She'll be happy to stand in if they need someone in front of the camera."

"Is that the girl I saw you with earlier?"

Alex nodded.

Lily shifted on the couch. *So, she works with him. How convenient.* She hoped a two-by-four would hit her in the head by accident.

Alex tilted his head. "You okay?"

Lily faked a smile. She was good at masking her emotions when it came to men while secretly seething underneath.

If he wants Miss High Heels, he can have her.

Alex placed her ankle on the couch and turned the ice pack over. "Alli's just my co-star on the show. There's nothing between us."

"Uh-huh." Lily jolted when the ice touched her tender ankle.

How had he guessed my thoughts so easily? It was unnerving.

"I'm being honest, Lil. I don't want her around."

"Who said you wanted her? Even if you did, I wouldn't care. It's not like we're together."

Something flashed across his eyes, and she could tell her words stung.

Well, good. Maybe we can both be uncomfortable now.

"Listen, I don't know what I did wrong." Alex touched her hand. "If I took things too fast the other night, I'm sorry. I want to help you."

She pulled her hand away. Maybe the pain was making her grumpy, but all she wanted was for Alex to leave. "If you want to be my friend, then I'd appreciate the space. Is that too much to ask?"

He paused and sat back, looking at her in that pained way psychologists do when they're about to sum up a patient's problem. "What are you so scared of?"

"What do you mean? I'm not scared."

Denial always had been her forte. She sat up straighter.

"I'm trying to help you, and you're pushing me away. If something is bothering you . . ."

"I don't know." Lily cringed at her inability to find some kind of clever comeback that might divert this conversation. She didn't want to push him away, not really, but she struggled to trust anyone after what had happened with Thomas.

Even this morning, Thomas had texted again, asking why she wouldn't talk to him, saying that he only wanted a few minutes alone with her.

She couldn't delete it fast enough.

"We can take it slow. I promise." Alex held up his hands.

"How do we take it slow when you're only here temporarily? I'm not going to be your long-distance girlfriend waiting for your next break. Can't you see that this won't work?"

"There are a thousand ways to make it possible. Visit LA. Meet me in between."

She really didn't want to talk about this, especially when her ankle was throbbing. "Alex, no. My life is here. If you haven't noticed yet, I have a business to run. My parents need my help. I can't just leave everything." She knew those were all surface reasons covering up her true motivation for not wanting to get involved with him. Thomas had betrayed her sense of trust, and there was no easy way to fix how deeply he had scarred her.

"Then what if I made it work?"

"What do you mean?"

He moved closer on the couch. "What if I gave up my life in

LA and moved back here? Started over. Would you change your mind then?"

Her mouth opened but no words came out, like her whole heart was about to crack open. "No, Alex."

He looked down at the ground. "We could make this work. Let me prove it to you."

"No. Don't even make this some sort of test I have to pass. I have enough pressure as it is. There's not time."

"There's always time."

"No, Alex. I'm seriously freaking out here because I've got so much to do in the next week, and I can't even walk now. And you're putting pressure on me? If I could leave right now, I would."

"Good thing you're stuck on the couch." He gave her a small smile that broke the tension.

"Not funny." She tried to suppress a smile. "Really, I don't know how I'm going to get ready for next week." She put her hands over her face, shielding herself from the pile of bills sitting in her kitchen. "I'm going to have to cancel the grand opening. That's all there is to it." Her eyes filled with tears, but she refused to let Alex see her cry.

"If you want to have the grand opening, I'll help you. We will get this thing off the ground."

"You don't know how to make truffles."

"Teach me. I offered to help before."

"You're a house flipper. What do you know about chocolate?"

"Absolutely nothing. But how different can it be from building a house? It's all about following steps."

She lowered her hands and wondered if he could see the doubt written all over her face. She ran her fingers through her hair. "I don't know, Alex."

"You have two options at this point. Either we work together and have the grand opening, or you cancel it. Your decision."

Lily exhaled some emotional steam. First she had agreed to renovate her house with him. Now he was going to help her make chocolates? How in the world would she keep her feelings in check?

She laid her head back on the couch, defeated. "Okay. If those are my options, then I want to pull off the grand opening. But as far as us—"

"You don't have to decide anything about us right now. You have a lot on your plate. Just focus on your grand opening. Come up with a list of tasks you need completed, and I'll start doing whatever you need—even making fudge. Just don't blame me if it turns out terrible."

"Not funny." Lily tried to get up from the couch but felt Alex's hand on her arm.

"Don't you dare." His eyes told her he wasn't kidding.

"I was trying to get my phone and make a to-do list."

"You're supposed to stay on the couch and rest your ankle."

She watched him retrieve the phone. A twinge of guilt twisted inside her. Had she been too hard on him? All he wanted to do was help.

"Anything else I can get you?" He handed her the phone. "I need to head next door, but I'm only a text away if you need something."

"Listen, Alex," she said slowly. "I'm really sorry if I came across a little strong earlier. It's not that I don't want your help. The problem is—"

"No, don't say it." He touched his index finger gently to her lips. "I don't want to talk about problems. I want to convince you that, even when there are obstacles, some things are worth fighting for."

Then he leaned forward and gave her forehead a kiss, so tender and light, the feeling swept through her whole body.

"Why don't you rest until I come back?"

She leaned back against the couch, still reeling from his kiss.

After she watched him walk out the door, she squeezed her eyes shut, as if she could squeeze every thought of him out of her mind.

This will never work.

In less than a month, he would be gone for good, and so would the dream that dangled in front of her. The whisper of a future she wanted so badly. The promise of love she would not let herself have.

CHAPTER SEVENTEEN

ALEX

W*hat have I gotten myself into?* As Alex pounded a nail into the wall, he kept replaying the conversation from the day before. He was *in deep.* Two houses to renovate. Now, a grand opening to pull off.

No problem.

He remembered his dad's words when he was a high school freshman, learning painful lessons about procrastination. After putting off studying for two tests and writing a paper, Alex had put his head down on his textbook one night and told his father, "I can't possibly get all of this done. I'm going to fail."

His dad had put his hand on his shoulder. "You know how you eat an elephant? One bite at a time."

Which was exactly what Alex needed to do right now.

He put down his hammer and walked over to Mike. "I'm heading to Lily's. Need to make some plans."

"How's the new girlfriend doing?"

"She's not my girlfriend." Alex wiped his hands on his pants. "Won't even consider it."

"I saw the way she looked at you. She's got it bad."

Alex rubbed the back of his neck. "How can you tell?"

"It's my sixth sense."

"How many times have you been wrong?"

Mike chuckled. "Maybe three or four, but sometimes women are tricky. They say one thing, think another."

"So, basically, you don't know." Alex grinned as he backed away from Mike.

On his way over, he passed Lily's sisters' cars in the driveway. He knocked and heard footsteps.

Megan opened the door. "Hey, Alex, come on in. Thanks for taking care of Lily yesterday when we were gone."

Lily was sprawled on the couch, her ankle wrapped in a cold pack.

"How's the patient today?" he asked.

"Not very patient." Cassidy sat on the floor next to Lily. "I tried to persuade her to sleep at Mom and Dad's, but she said this couch was more comfortable. The only problem is that she won't stay off her foot."

Lily shrugged. "They're making plans for the grand opening, and I'm trying to explain that I can't pull them off. Not like this." She pointed toward her swollen ankle.

Megan joined Cass on the floor, scrolling through her phone. "We told her that chocolate isn't enough. She needs some music and decorations."

"Add some candles and lots of glitz, and it will be perfect." Cassidy clapped her hands.

"That sounds like a middle school birthday party." Lily rubbed her temples.

"Cassidy is great at decorating." Megan put her phone down. "She won't go crazy with the sparkly stuff. Let her take over the decorations, and I'll do the promos. We'll make sure everyone in town shows up."

"But it's so late. I should have been promoting it two weeks ago."

"It doesn't matter when you start." Megan walked toward Lily and sat on the arm of the couch. "It's all about attracting the person who has never stepped foot in your shop."

"Meg's right," Alex added. "This week is the critical time. If it helps, I'll put the word out."

"Speaking of Wild Harbor, have you seen the latest gossip?" Megan gave Lily a look.

Alex glanced from Megan to Lily to Cassidy. "I have no idea what you're talking about."

Megan showed him her phone. "Somebody took a photo of you and Alli at the coffee shop."

Alex exhaled as he sat next to Lily. "I should have known better than to go to a public place with Alli."

"You can't hide anything." Megan stood. "You're the talk of the town right now. Too bad we can't get that same sort of excitement around Lily's event."

Cassidy's eyes brightened. "I have an idea. You need to be seen together on a date. Give people something to talk about before the grand opening—"

"No," Lily interrupted. "I don't want people taking pictures of us, especially when I'm in the middle of eating, then blasting it to the world."

Megan leaned against the wall, crossing her arms. "Cass is right. Publicity, even when it's bad, is still publicity. This would be great for your event!"

Cassidy clapped and let out a squeal. "Yes, people will show up just to see if you two are a couple. Since Alex is planning on attending the grand opening anyway, the date just creates more buzz. Then the grand opening gets them in the door."

"That's terribly tacky." Lily shook her head and buried her face in her hands. "I'm not faking a relationship."

"It doesn't have to be more than it appears." Alex pulled her hands down so he could see her face. "Even hanging out at a coffee shop is enough fodder for the gossip mill in this town."

"I'm not stooping to deceit." Lily's expression told him she was done with this conversation.

"You're the boss, but I'll tell you this." Alex leaned toward her, locking eyes. "At some point, you decide if your business is worth it. It's been floundering for months, not because you don't make great chocolate, but because people have yet to try it. They might not get a chance to, if you're not willing to do everything you can."

He wasn't trying to twist her arm, but she needed to hear some tough love. She couldn't let her pride get in the way.

Lily sat up, a fire in her eyes. "For your information, I am willing to do whatever it takes. I just hate pretending, so that people think—"

" . . . we're a couple?" he finished.

"So what?" Megan threw her hands in the air. "If it makes your business a success, I'd do it in a second."

"Me too." Cassidy turned to her sister. "Desperate times call for desperate measures."

"You guys think I'm desperate?" Lily asked.

Her sisters nodded in unison.

Lily covered her face and moaned.

"I don't think it can hurt." Cassidy touched Lily's arm. "We need everything going for you, and I mean *everything*. Alex's appearance will help, but you need long-term customers. We can plan the best party in the world, but if you don't get enough sales, you might have to close your shop. That's the last thing I want for you."

"Me too," Megan added. "We'll do whatever you want, but you should consider building some excitement before the event. That's all."

Lily looked between her sisters, then fell back into the couch with a sigh. "Okay, you win. I'll do whatever it takes."

Megan gave Lily a high five. "You won't regret this."

Cassidy turned to Alex. "I have the perfect idea. Tomorrow night there's an outdoor concert at the park. It's a country rock band that sings love ballads. It would be the perfect place to get some buzz going."

Alex looked at Lily, who was frowning.

"That means I'll have to go on crutches. Not exactly ideal for a concert."

"No," said Cassidy. "But it will be perfect for gaining community sympathy."

Lily crossed her arms. "I don't want sympathy. I just want—"

"Sales. We know," Megan said. "But this would be the easiest place to be seen with Alex. All you have to do is hang out. If it's just the two of you on a blanket, people will talk . . . and that's all you need."

Alex leaned toward Lily. "Are you okay with this? I don't want you to feel awkward."

"I'm not sure I have a choice." Then her face softened. "Don't get me wrong, I'm thankful you're willing to do this. I know I can't repay you for everything you've done for me."

He smiled. "You don't have to repay me for anything." He stood and headed to the door. "See you tomorrow for the concert?"

She nodded as Alex closed the door behind him.

He needed time to think through this.

Maybe Lily was right, and this was a terrible idea.

But if it was, then why did he want it so badly?

CHAPTER EIGHTEEN

LILY

"Everyone is staring at us." Lily gripped her crutches as she hobbled alongside Alex toward the outdoor atrium.

At least the weather was cooperating for the evening concert. The sky looked like it had been painted by a French impressionist, all hazy purples and pinks.

Making their way across the lawn, just past the perennial garden, people who had arrived early gawked as Alex walked by.

She had always liked being part of Wild Harbor, a place where everyone not only knew you, but also knew your parents and your grandparents. Now, she had the feeling she was being talked about behind her back, the same as when she had given her book report in the fifth grade and worn hand-me-down burnt-orange corduroy pants which were slightly out of style.

She wanted to run and hide.

"Why don't we sit under that tree?" Alex pointed toward a large oak at the back of the lawn. "We should have a good view of the band, and it won't be quite as loud."

"You don't want to be closer?"

"Not unless you do."

"Oh, no, I already feel like I'm on display—the crippled woman who's a sympathy date for the hunk on TV."

"Okay, first of all you're not a cripple or a sympathy date. You're gorgeous, and every man here can see that. Secondly, I've never heard you call me a hunk, so I guess that's good?" He gave her a teasing grin.

"That's what they call you. *The home renovation hunk.* It's why your dating life makes the gossip headlines."

"I don't care about the gossip, Lily." He looked at her with his blue eyes, then turned to walk toward the tree.

How could she not fall for those eyes? He hooked her every time he looked her way or touched her hand. She wondered how long she'd be able to hide what she was feeling for him.

As they made their way to the tree, a young girl, who Lily guessed was not more than eight, approached Alex. "Can I get your autograph?"

Her mom stood a few feet away and gave her daughter an encouraging nod.

"Sure. What's your name?"

"Bella."

Alex pulled out a small flyer and a pen. "Well, Bella, do you like chocolate?" He asked as he signed the flyer.

"Yes."

"Tell your mom that I'm going to be at Lily's Chocolate Shop. Here's a flyer with the date and time. I signed it so you remember to come."

The girl looked at the paper. "Thank you! I can't wait to go to this. I'm going to tell my mom right now!" She ran back to her mom and held out the flyer.

Lily turned to look at him incredulously. "Where did you get that flyer? I didn't have time to make that."

"Oh, I have my ways." He gave her a quick smile. "And I have an assistant who can send things to any printer in the country. I thought we could hand them out tonight, or in this case, sign as autographs."

"Aren't you sneaky."

"Not sneaky. Just smart."

"I feel like my head's not been on straight since I fell. I'm lucky to have you helping."

"I want you to forget what you have to do and just enjoy tonight. Promise?"

"I'll try. But it's hard when all these people keep staring at us. How do you do this every day? It would drive me crazy."

"I'm not really that famous in LA. Not compared to the big movie stars. For most people, I'm just a normal guy."

Yeah, right. Alex had never been a normal guy.

He spread the blanket under the tree. "I love what I do. But some days, I wonder if I missed out by not staying here."

"What do you mean?"

He took her hand and helped her sit on the blanket. "There's something really special about people knowing your name and where you came from. A place to put down roots and raise a family. Not to mention, you're here."

Before she could respond, Lily heard a voice behind her. "Excuse me. My name is Tim, and I'm from *The Wild Harbor News.* I wondered if I could take your picture for the event?"

Lily looked at Alex and started to giggle. *If this was what it was like to be famous, she'd never survive.*

"Sure, on one condition." Alex gave the photographer a warm smile. "Only if you mention this event in Wild Harbor." He handed Tim the flyer with the grand opening information.

"Okay." Tim nodded, then pointed to Alex and Lily. "If you two could move closer together—"

Lily leaned toward Alex as he scooted closer to her. Her back was touching his arm, and she could feel his breath on her neck as he looked over her shoulder. A part of her wanted to lean into him, to let herself relax in his arms. But instead, she was holding her breath, trying not to let him feel her tension at his closeness.

"A little more," the photographer said, motioning for them to move closer.

"This guy must think we're on a date or something," Lily whispered. She angled her body into his, leaning into his chest, the warmth of his skin against hers.

"What's wrong with that?" Alex whispered back, his breath in her ear.

Nothing. Nothing at all.

DURING THE FIRST half of the concert and throughout intermission, people kept interrupting Alex, asking him to sign autographs or take pictures. When the second half of the concert started, he asked Lily to go for a walk in the perennial gardens nearby.

As they strolled under a flower-covered pergola, the sunset tinged everything in a warm glow, and the garden offered an escape from the crowds. The scent from the blooming perennials was intoxicating, and the bushes planted around the edge gave them privacy.

Since most of the people were watching the band, they had the garden to themselves—just the two of them—on an evening that dripped in color and fragrance.

"You know, I could get used to this." Alex tilted his head and admired the pink night sky.

"What do you mean?" Lily gripped her crutches as she maneuvered the brick path. They found a garden bench tucked into a private corner surrounded by azalea bushes.

"Spending time with you in a garden while the sun sets," he said, sitting down.

"I'm sure LA has gorgeous nights too." She joined him and set her crutches aside.

"Yes, it does. But you're not in LA."

"Alex, you could have any woman you wanted."

He stopped and turned toward her. "Not any. I can't have you." He brushed his hand across her cheek.

Lily closed her eyes for a moment. "You're making it hard to just be friends."

"Maybe that's the idea."

"We can't keep pretending this could work."

"Because I don't live here? I could change that."

"I don't want you to change for me—"

"I could move back. Give up the show. Start a business here."

"Then what happens when it doesn't work out? I can't let you do that. Being on TV is what you've always dreamed about."

"What I've always dreamed about is *you*. Remember how I tried to kiss you on the porch swing? I thought I must be the most repulsive creature ever when you refused me."

"I wasn't repulsed. I thought you were kissing me for all the wrong reasons."

"If I could go back to that moment, I'd tell you I was crazy for you, and I'm sorry I ever took Priscilla to the prom."

Lily shook her head. "But you didn't say that. I had no idea what you felt."

"I thought you hated me."

"I thought you were using me."

He paused. "What did we know about love? Or anything really?"

"I'm not sure I know much about love now," she said, looking away.

He took her face in his hands and tilted it toward him.

"Alex, we can't—" She had started to put up the walls, listing all the reasons why it wouldn't work, how the distance was too much, how her past haunted her.

Instead, he wrapped his arms around her and began to kiss her, the warmth of his lips melting the past. His fingers were in her hair, her body angled into his.

She felt like she was drowning, swept away by waves she couldn't control, pulled under by a force too strong to fight against. She wanted to stay in Alex's arms, to lose control of her emotions, to let herself love him.

But even now, the memory of Thomas's face appeared, the outline of his clenched jaw, his hand grabbing her arm, the shot of pain from his grip, then stinging humiliation. Why did he haunt her when she was finally rid of him?

Alex was nothing like Thomas. He would never hurt her or betray her trust, would he? The doubt was a passing shadow, a dark cloud drifting across the sun. But the cold dread weighed heavy on her heart, enough to make her wrench free from Alex's embrace.

"No, I can't—" She leaned away from him, the fear of what it would mean to love him—to lose him—crushing her breath.

"Lily, I'm willing to make this work, whatever it takes. I'll move here and schedule my show around our lives. Whatever you need me to do to prove this to you. We've known each other our whole lives. I want to be with you—"

Something inside her wanted her to run. Except she couldn't. She looked down at her swollen ankle, angry that her body had failed her.

"You don't understand. I can't just get over what happened with Thomas. I can't be with anyone right now. Not even you."

She hadn't meant for the words to come out so cruelly.

As soon as she said it, hurt tinged his eyes. His hands fell to his sides, letting her go. He took a step back, his face fallen. "If that's what you want—"

That's not what I want. Oh, please, no.

It was all she could do to restrain herself from asking his

forgiveness. From opening herself up to love. But she had made it clear.

In his kindness, he was giving her exactly what she asked for, even though it killed her inside.

Her phone buzzed in her pocket, the sound startling her back into the moment.

Megan. She didn't want to answer—her voice would betray her. Lily put the phone back in her pocket. A message came through again, almost immediately.

Megan: Pick up the phone. It's an emergency.

Had her father fallen again? Did he have another stroke?
She looked at Alex. "It's Megan. She needs me to call."

Alex's hurt changed to concern for her. "Of course. Call her back."

She held her breath, waiting for Megan to pick up.

"Lily, I'm so sorry to interrupt your date." Megan sounded breathless.

"What's happened? Is it Dad?"

"No, Dad's fine."

Lily breathed a sigh of relief.

"I picked up the party supplies and swung by your shop to drop them off. That's when I noticed the place had been broken into."

"What? How? Megan, are you okay?"

"Whoever did it left before I got there. But the shop is—I'm sorry to tell you this, but it's a mess. Tables overturned. Glass on the floor. I think they stole your cash."

Lily put her fingers up to her temples, the pressure building behind her forehead as she tried to keep from crying. Her voice quivered. "I'll be right there."

Alex looked at her, trying to decipher what had happened. "What's going on?" he whispered.

"Do you know how much cash you had?" Megan asked.

"Not much. The one thing about being poor is there isn't much to steal."

"Oh, Lily, you always look on the bright side. We'll get this cleared up."

"I'm on my way." She ended the call and looked at Alex, the tears beginning to stream. "My shop was broken into. They took the cash and wrecked the place. Do you mind taking me over there?"

Alex stepped toward her, his face softening.

She could tell he was restraining himself, holding back from touching her, afraid of how she might react.

"I'm so sorry, Lily."

She wanted him to touch her. To hold her in his arms.

His apology broke the last of her resolve.

The tears spiraled down her face as she stepped forward, wrapping her arms around him, hoping he would do the same. She needed his unspoken reassurance that this would work out somehow, and she would not have to close the business.

It had been so long since she had felt like something was going her way. Now she had just rejected the man who had promised to give up everything for her.

What had she done?

Alex wrapped his arms around her tightly. He didn't say anything, but in his silent embrace, he was holding her up, not physically, but emotionally, giving her something she desperately needed in that moment.

"It's going to be okay," he whispered, his cheek resting against the side of her head, his soft words brushing her ear.

If she hadn't been so distraught, she would have reveled in his closeness. But all she could do was let the tears fall and hang on to him, grasping for some assurance. She needed to know that even when life was at its worst, there was still hope.

CHAPTER NINETEEN

ALEX

The damage was done, in more ways than one. Alex wasn't thinking of the shop's damage, although that was certainly a mess. He was haunted by Lily's words in the garden: *I can't be with anyone right now. Not even you.*

The last phrase inflicted the most pain, like the turning of a knife.

He had tried to set the hurt aside when they had gone to the shop and surveyed the damage from the thief. Glass shattered on the floor from where they'd broken through the back door. Ceramic plates smashed on her new tile. Tables overturned. Chairs upended.

The shop looked like Alex felt, badly damaged.

Lily walked through the broken pieces littered across the floor, carefully avoiding the shards with her crutches.

"But why?" she asked. "Why would someone target my shop? I can barely pay my bills as it is."

Megan wrapped her arms around her sister in a side hug.

"I'm so sorry. Some people are just jerks. I'm so thankful you weren't here. Can you imagine?"

Lily shuddered. "I can't even go there in my mind. It's too terrifying. Maybe God is sending me a sign."

Megan looked at her sister. "Don't even say that. Bad things happen to good people all the time. Our family isn't being punished as some sort of *sign*. It's just the result of living in a broken world."

"Broken is right." Lily surveyed the mess. "One more thing to do before the grand opening."

"I do have a piece of good news. The cash is still there. They didn't take it."

"What? But why would they break into the shop?"

"I don't know. It seems odd." Megan picked up one of the shards. "You haven't seen any strange people coming into the shop, right?"

"Not that I know of."

Alex noticed a look cross Lily's face, like she was thinking of something.

"Something wrong?" Alex asked quietly.

She shook her head. "It's nothing."

At that moment, Matt tore into the shop, stopping when he saw the damage. "I got here as fast as I could." He shook his head in disbelief. "I can't believe what a mess they made. I thought when people break in, they're looking for cash or valuable items. What's the point of destroying property?"

Cassidy came in next, with Cameron behind her. "Oh, Lily," Cassidy gazed at the destruction, as she hugged her sister. "I called Cameron to help. I hope you don't mind."

Cameron picked up a toppled chair. "I'm sorry, Lily. I can bring a crew of guys here tomorrow to help clean up. Have you called the police yet?"

"I should do that now." Lily pulled out her phone as

Cameron, Cassidy, and Matt looked for evidence. Her hands shook a bit as she looked at the screen and froze.

"Do you want me to do it?" Alex put his hand on her arm.

She shook her head, her eyes wide with fear.

If there was any way he could fix this situation, he would. The thought of leaving town, after her shop had been broken into, left him uneasy.

"You should go. My family can take care of this."

"No, I'll stay until you leave. Tomorrow, I'm going to check on you to make sure you're okay."

"Really, you don't have to," she said, her eyes soft and sad. "I'll be fine."

"I'll be there at seven."

She gave him a weary smile. "I'm so sorry our evening was ruined."

"No apologies," he whispered and gave her a hug.

She held on longer than he expected, her arms locked around him tightly, begging for some reassurance.

If only I could give you more.

She slowly pulled away, giving him one final look, before making the phone call she dreaded. "I'd like to report a crime . . ."

As ALEX PULLED up the next morning, Lily was already coming out the door, making her way on crutches down the long sidewalk.

"Hey," she said quietly as he met her halfway. "A man of your word, huh?" She checked her watch.

"Always. You okay?"

She shrugged. "Matt's arranged a cleanup crew at the shop today. A few small things are missing—my spare key and some cooking tools—but I think I left them in the wrong place."

"You're going on crutches?"

"Well, this is the best I can do. My ankle is feeling a little better today, even if the rest of me feels a little bruised."

Same here.

"I know this is bad timing, but the crew needs to start on your home today. We don't need you there right now, but I wanted you to know."

"Oh." She slapped her forehead. "I completely forgot."

"Lily, if today doesn't work—"

"No, no. Go ahead. I might as well have one good thing happening in my life. If we can turn this house around, then maybe everything will turn around, right?"

She was trying to be positive, but her eyes looked sad, and he wondered if she'd slept last night.

"Not to sound like your sisters, but don't forget to keep your weight off the ankle today. I want you to be healed for the grand opening."

"I'm sure they will remind me constantly. Cass begged me not to come, but I told them I wasn't staying away."

"That's because she cares."

"I know. My whole family is worried about me."

"For what it's worth, I'm worried about you too."

She looked at him and paused, like she wanted to say something, but couldn't. "Well, I probably should get to the shop." She gave him a weak smile, then climbed into her car.

He closed the door and gave a small wave as she drove off.

She might not let him stay in her world, but when he left town, she would have a beautiful place to call home. She could sit on the back porch and watch the sun set over the water, with someone next to her, while the tide lapped the shore.

But that someone would not be him. She had made her feelings clear.

Not even me.

As much as he tried to forget, her words played an awful looping soundtrack in his mind.

~

As ALEX WALKED UP to the salvage shop's well-worn door, he hoped Joshua would be there. Even though he had only met the man once, he sensed he knew more than he let on, though he had no idea why.

This is crazy.

He stopped, afraid he had misjudged him. Maybe he was expecting too much. He had the tendency to do that. To project all his expectations on someone then face disappointment when they didn't live up to them. It was a weakness, but he didn't know how to stop doing it, like picking at a scab that just wouldn't heal.

Alex slowly turned the handle and pushed the door open with a squeak.

The shop sat in stillness. Fragments from the past waited in dusty darkness, hiding stories from families long gone.

Alex stepped in and cleared his throat. The sound echoed in the silence. Light from a faint window seeped into the dusty air, one long glowing strip slicing into the darkness.

"Hello? Joshua?"

Silence.

Alex sighed. He had gotten his hopes up—and for what? A shop full of old memories?

In the corner, he saw the window Lily had selected. It had been carefully wrapped in a blanket for protection with one corner peeking out, glittering in the light.

Alex approached it, his footsteps echoing across the wood floor. He knelt and slowly unwrapped it. As the blanket fell away, he saw the stained glass. The first time he had seen it, he hadn't really looked at the picture clearly. Maybe he had been too distracted by Joshua's presence or had his mind made up against the idea. Now that he was alone, he could inspect the details

A white figure in the center was actually two doves that appeared to overlap in the air. He studied it for a minute, wondering who had made it and what it meant. As his finger traced the birds across the dusty glass, he heard the familiar squeak of the door and turned to see Joshua's slow figure enter the building.

"I'm sorry." Alex almost lost his balance as he stood quickly, feeling guilty for trespassing in Joshua's shop. "The door was open, so I came in, thinking you were here. I wanted to pick up the window."

Joshua shook his head. "I saw you come in. I knew I needn't worry."

His serene face held an expression Alex couldn't read.

"We're starting to work on Lily's house, and she's had some setbacks this week. I thought if I could surprise her with the new window, it might cheer her up."

"Changed your mind, then?"

"I guess. It's construction. We make things work, whether it's easy or not."

"Sounds a lot like people. Trying to force things to work from their own strength." Joshua stopped and looked at Alex, his smile like the warm glow of a candle.

Alex had no idea what this had to do with the window. "Yeah, I've been guilty of that," he admitted.

Joshua took a brass door handle and started polishing it. "Did you figure out what's on the window? Children see it right away. You don't even have to tell them. It's the adults that are too blind to see it."

"I didn't the first time. But when I came back today, it

jumped out at me—two doves." He traced the outline with his fingers.

"Two?" Joshua questioned.

"Depending on how you look at it. They almost merge into one shape in the sky. It's both."

Joshua nodded. "The window was designed by a man who had it made for his fiancé. They were building a new home on Market Street, and the window was created as a wedding present. But a year later, she drowned in the lake and the man, who was grief stricken, had the window removed from his home because it was too painful to look at.

"A few years later, the man remarried, and their marriage was a long and happy one. On their twenty-fifth anniversary, the woman surprised him with a gift she had found in a shop, long forgotten.

"When the man opened it, he was shocked to see the same window he had designed for his first wife. After all these years, the man finally understood why he had needed to let it go, and how it had brought him joy to find it again. Pain and joy always work together."

Alex put his hand on the cool glass, the white of the doves flying into the air, the pink and ruby red sky beneath. "But what does that mean? I thought the doves represented his love and how he had to let go."

"Ah, yes. Perhaps. But there was more too, and now he could see that. He had lost someone dear to him, but he had also found love again."

"I'm not sure if Lily will find it comforting or will think it's creepy that he got his window back."

"Depends on whether you see it as coincidence or redemption." Joshua turned to Alex. "Like most things in life, it's all perspective."

"I came here to get a window. But I feel like you might have some advice for me—about Lily."

Joshua chuckled. "I've already given you advice, son. Didn't you hear it?" Then he turned and walked away.

"Wait a minute," said Alex. "I don't know what you mean—and I haven't paid you yet."

The man turned at the door. "It's on the house." Then he stepped outside and slipped away.

CHAPTER TWENTY

ALEX

Over a week passed before Alex saw Lily again. He had been busy working on her home and only asked her to come in for a quick shoot in the afternoon, so they could paint the living room on camera.

It was one of the few tasks Lily loved, even if she ended up covered in paint by the end.

But instead of their normal easygoing conversation, they painted the walls light gray in awkward silence. What little they did say seemed forced.

Alli walked over, her arms crossed. "Is something wrong between you two?"

Lily shook her head.

Alex furrowed his brow. "No, why?"

"Well, for what it's worth, you're acting like you can't stand each other. Standing far apart. Avoiding each other. You guys need to turn up the chemistry on camera."

Then she turned to Lily. "With a guy as handsome as him, it shouldn't be hard."

Lily's face flushed with heat as Alli walked away.

"Don't listen to her. You did fine." Alex wiped his hands on a towel, then reached over and wiped the tip of her nose. "By the way, you're cute with paint on your nose."

She made a face and wiped the spot with the back of her hand. "I don't think my customers will appreciate it if I'm covered in paint. Sorry to leave you in the middle of this project, but I need to get back and make more chocolates for the grand opening."

"Anything I can do to help?" He put down his paintbrush.

Lily paused. "Not unless you want to learn to make chocolates. No pressure, though."

"I offered to help before, as long as I get to sample the final product."

"Free samples are how I'm paying you, in case you didn't know."

"Sounds like a deal. Let me finish up things here, and I'll be right over."

When he arrived at the shop, Lily was already dressed in an apron, sitting on a stool to rest her ankle. She wasn't using her crutches anymore since her ankle was healing well.

"I thought maybe you bailed on me. Got chicken."

"Nope. I'm up for the challenge. Just don't get angry if I make a mess."

"I won't be angry, but I might hand you a mop." She gave him a playful smile.

As far as he was concerned, she could make any mundane task sound good. He slipped on an apron over his T-shirt while Lily glanced his way.

"It's not your usual look, but the apron looks good on you." She started to climb off the stool.

He stopped her with his hands. "Don't get down. You're not supposed to be putting weight on your ankle all the time."

"The doctor said I can for short periods."

"Aren't you glad I made you go to the doctor? How much have you been on your feet today?"

She gave him a guilty look. "Probably more than I should have."

"Ah, the truth comes out. Tell me what you need, and I'll go get it."

"Just those utensils." She pointed to the counter, where a few kitchen tools were scattered. "We're going to be melting chocolates tonight. But I need to move closer to the stovetop so I can make sure the temperature and chocolate consistency stay even." She started to move off her stool before Alex noticed she was trying to put weight on her foot again.

"No way," he said. "That's my job, remember? At least let me help you get there." He pushed her on the stool over to the stovetop and handed her the spatula.

"Ah, yes, the consistency of the chocolate is almost perfect. Now, I need the truffles from the fridge in the back. There are two large trays we have to dip."

He brought out both trays and set them before her. Without their chocolate coating, they looked rather disappointing. "No offense, but they don't look like much."

"But they will eventually, and the flavors are incredible. They're rather plain right now, but once we coat them in chocolate, each type will be unique." She pointed to each flavor. "This one is raspberry dark chocolate topped with a raspberry garnish. My favorite is the mocha truffle, crowned with a coffee bean. I also make a coconut truffle coated in dark chocolate with white stripes. The caramel truffle is filled with a soft liquid caramel covered with a chocolate metallic gold sheen. My most popular is a peanut butter truffle, topped with a few peanuts and a touch of sea salt. I'd let you try one, but they're better dipped in chocolate."

"I'll take your word for it."

"Watch carefully as I show you how this is done." Lily gingerly took a truffle off the tray and slowly dipped it into the melted chocolate with a circular dipping tool that allowed the chocolate to drop off the bottom. Then she pulled the tool up, letting the excess drip off the truffle into the bowl. She placed the confection on another tray so that the chocolate could harden into a shell.

"See? It's easy. Your turn."

Alex took the dipping tool and attempted to dip a truffle into the chocolate, but it fell into the hot mixture. "Oh, sorry."

"It can be salvaged. Let me help." She took his hand and guided it to the chocolate and helped him scoop it in one quick motion. "Now, give it a few gentle taps to shed the excess."

He whacked the tool on the side of the pot, which sent chocolate splattering across the stovetop and the truffle flying. It landed on the countertop.

Lily covered her mouth and started laughing. "Not quite so hard. Otherwise, they're like bouncy balls. Flying everywhere."

"Sorry. I didn't know my own strength." He gave her his most apologetic look.

A smile played across her lips. "We'll donate that one to our volunteers."

As she picked up the ruined truffle, Alex furrowed his brow and asked, "Who might that be?"

"You." She held the chocolate up to his mouth. "Take a bite."

He slowly bit into the chocolate as the truffle melted in his mouth. "Wow. That is amazing," he said between bites.

The chocolate mocha interior was a mixture of rich flavors, with the sweet chocolate countering the slightly bitter depth of the espresso. He took another bite, his lips barely grazing her chocolate-coated fingers. If he could, he would have kissed the chocolate right off her fingertips. Instead, he stopped himself, afraid to show what he was really thinking.

"You have melted chocolate on your mouth. Let me help."
She took her finger and wiped his mouth. Then she stared at
him for a long moment.

Maybe it was the chocolate. Or the fact that she was so close,
he could feel her breath across his skin. No longer did she have
that distant, closed-off look in her eyes or the staunch walls she
put up to keep him from getting too close. Something had
bloomed in her, the slow unfurling of trust, and he felt the invitation before she leaned in slightly and closed her eyes.

"What are you doing?" he whispered as her lips drew to his.
"I thought you said—"

But her kiss quieted him as she gently pressed her lips to his.
He couldn't think, he couldn't breathe. He knew he should stop,
but everything about it felt right.

Stop. Just stop.

He pulled away from her.

Lily looked at him confused. "I don't know what came
over me."

"Why are you doing this to me?" He closed his eyes. Any
more of this and he'd lose control. "You told me you can't be
with me. But your actions say something totally different."

She hesitated, weighing her words. "I know. It's just—"

"It's what? You need to just say it." If she would tell him that
there was any chance for them to be together, Alex would drop
everything for her. But he needed her to say it.

"I can't."

"It infuriates me that you toy with my emotions, Lily."

"I'm not toying—"

"Then how do you explain what happened just now?"

"I don't know." She put her hands over her face.

"You don't know?" He laughed in disbelief as he shook his
head. "Do you always kiss guys and not know why?"

"No, I don't just kiss anyone . . ." She stumbled over her
words as she ran her hands through her hair. "You want to

know the truth?" Her eyes held a stormy mix of fire and desire. "Because when I'm with you, I want to be more than friends. But I can't be. And for a second, I forgot all the reasons why. It was . . . a momentary lapse of judgment. That's all. Are you happy now?"

Her walls were up, pushing him away again. He didn't know how much more rejection he could take. "Maybe it would be better if I left." He started to walk out.

"Alex."

He kept walking away even as she pleaded with him.

"Alex, please don't . . ."

He stopped, unable to face her. "Give me one reason not to leave." He waited for her answer as the silence in the shop echoed in his ears.

"Because," she paused as her voice quivered with emotion. "I need you. I can't do this without you."

He turned and saw the longing in her eyes. He couldn't walk out the door. "I'll do it on one condition. You can't kiss me like that again, understand? It makes things complicated between us. You can't get my hopes up, then keep dashing them. I need you to stay away."

Lily nodded in silence.

He walked back to the stovetop, trying to forget what had just happened. *As if I can.*

Some guys would gladly kiss a girl with no commitment, but he wasn't the type who could date a girl without his whole heart involved. If Lily had given him any hope of being together, he would do everything in his power to convince her it could work.

Now, he was questioning why he was even here. *Why did I come back to Wild Harbor if it only means more hurt?*

He had thought this visit might bring healing, but it was tearing him apart. He needed to finish the job. Say his goodbyes. Bury the past.

Because once he left for good, he couldn't come back and risk seeing her with someone else. Not even if it wrecked him to lose her again.

CHAPTER TWENTY-ONE

LILY

Lily woke with a vague sense of dread, the same feeling as when dental appointments loomed in front of her.

Alex was on the final stretch of completing her home, which she wasn't allowed to see until the end. She had done her part, showing up for camera shots of her working on her home. During the process, she had learned a lot of skills from Alex. He had been so patient, teaching her how to patch holes, lay flooring, and put up a tile backsplash.

Why would she ever let this man go?

He was saving her business and her life. What did she give to him in return? Nothing.

She lay in the dark bedroom, a slight feeling of nausea washing over her. It wasn't just the grand opening this evening. It was the thought of Alex being there while she tried to appear like nothing had happened between them. As if that kiss had been a mere lapse of judgment, instead of revealing her true feelings.

She wasn't even sure what had gotten into her. Old Lily would never have been that brave. *Or stupid.*

A soft knock came from the other side of her door. Megan peeked her head into the room. "Hey, did I wake you? Thought I'd stop by on my way to the newspaper office."

"No. I woke myself. Bad dreams."

Megan sat on the edge of the bed. Her black hair was curled around her shoulders, and she wore a striking deep-red blouse that flattered her brown eyes. Lily couldn't understand why every man in town wasn't trying to date her sister. She hovered on the edge of extremely gorgeous, the type that men took a second look at, even if Megan didn't acknowledge it or even care. Her excuses for not dating sounded all too familiar to Lily—fiercely independent, focused on making it as a journalist and building her career. Most people in town couldn't see Megan for what she was: a talented and savvy young professional determined to make it on her own terms, not the little girl from Wild Harbor who once had to be rescued from the undertow when she was seven.

"I stopped by to see how dad was. Late night, huh? Mom said she didn't hear you come in until three a.m."

"Yes. I finished all the chocolates last night. Good thing, since the opening is tonight."

"Did Alex stay?"

"Until the end."

"He's a saint. I don't know why you don't marry him right now."

"He deserves someone better than me." Lily leaned her head back.

"That is not true, and you know it."

"I haven't treated him well. Oh, Megan, I'm embarrassed to tell you what happened. I've been cruel to him."

"I'm sure you haven't."

"I told him I couldn't be with him, and he should leave me

alone. Just be my friend. You know how he responded? He did exactly what I asked. He let me go. The man was nothing but honorable, and I treated him horribly in return."

Tears streamed down her cheeks while Megan wrapped her arms around her. She could barely get the words out between her sobs. "I'm not dating material. What Thomas did to me—he made me afraid of every man who even looks twice at me."

"Thomas was a jerk to you. I wish Alex would pop him across the jaw. Or even better, I'd like to."

"What's worse is that I trust Alex completely, yet I can't even let myself get close to him. I'm so afraid—" She stumbled to complete her sentence, the sobs catching in her throat.

"You can't blame yourself for what Thomas did to you." Megan leaned her head against Lily's. "It's not your fault."

"I know that, but to take it out on Alex? It's wrong."

"You can still make this right. Just explain it to him."

"What do you mean? I did explain it."

"There's still time to tell Alex how you feel."

"No, I've ruined everything."

"Oh, Lily, you always did look at everything like a glass half empty. You can tell him tonight, after the grand opening."

"He's leaving soon. I don't want to date a guy who's famous and living across the country."

"Lily, stop." Megan held Lily's shoulders so she could look in her eyes. "You don't have to figure out the next ten years of your life. You only need to do the next right thing."

Lily closed her eyes. "But what is the next right thing?"

Megan sighed, as if she'd explained this a million times before and Lily was too thick-skulled to understand. "Remember when we were kids and we'd come home from school with some earth-shattering problem? Remember what Mom would do? She'd start singing hymns."

"You're not going to sing, are you? Because you might as well send Mom up here."

LOVE AT WILD HARBOR

Meg shook her head. "Nope. But my point is this. It was never the song that made me feel better. It was the realization I didn't have to figure it out on my own. You're not alone in this."

A knock sounded at the door as Mom slowly came in. "Lily? I brought breakfast in bed for the big day." She was holding a take-out bag and a coffee.

"Just for the record, you never did that for me when I lived here," Megan said.

"That's because Alex dropped these off. He said there's a note inside." She handed her the bag and gave a wink. "Enjoy."

Mom left the room while Megan eyed the bag. "Aren't you going to open it?"

"You're welcome to have some." Lily handed the coffee to Meg.

"No, I meant the note. I want to know what it says."

"It's private," Lily said, pulling out the paper.

"What? Are we in middle school or something? Just read it."

Lily opened the note carefully and made something up. "He asked, 'Do you like me? Circle yes or no.'"

"He did not write that. Give me that." She swiped the letter from Lily's hands and began reading out loud. "'Congrats on the big day. I'll be there cheering you on. This is your moment, a chance for everyone in Wild Harbor to see how amazing you are (and you truly are). I wouldn't say it if I didn't believe it. P.S. I thought you might need some coffee this morning after our late night. Love, Alex.'"

Megan dropped the letter on the bed and leaned back on Lily's pillows. "Now if that isn't a confession of his feelings, I don't know what is. To think that a guy like Alex would write that to *you*."

"Thanks, but you're really not making me feel any better."

"What do you mean?"

"That's exactly why I don't want to date him."

Another voice echoed from the hall. "Who?" Cassidy asked as she entered the room.

"Alex," Megan answered quickly.

Cassidy, dressed in a dreamy green blouse with black jeans and a black hat, looked as stunning as Megan.

"What are you doing here?" Lily moved to the edge of her bed, annoyed that her sisters always seemed to know more about her love life than she did.

"What do you mean? I'm here for your big day."

"I'd rather not be reminded." Lily stood. "I'm already nervous about it."

"Oh my goodness, it's going to be *huge.*" Cassidy flung her arms out. "I have all the flowers loaded in my trunk to decorate. Everyone is talking about Alex being there."

"That's probably why they'll all come. They just want to see *him.*"

"So what if they do?" Megan interjected. "If it means sales for you, then you've succeeded. That's what it's about, right?"

"I guess." Lily sounded uncertain.

"You've worked weeks on this and all you can say is 'I guess'?"

"Maybe it's just me, but I don't feel optimistic about tonight. I feel like I'm desperate. That I'm willing to use one of the nicest guys I've ever met for his fame, so I can pay the bills for a few months. What kind of person does that?" Lily flopped back onto the bed next to Megan.

"Lily, don't be so hard on yourself." Cassidy sat next to her. "People pay money to have celebrities at their events. That's not wrong. It's just business."

"That's exactly why it feels wrong." Lily curled up. "Alex is my friend. I care about him and all I've done for him is —nothing."

"He doesn't see it that way," Cassidy said.

"Well, I do. There must be something wrong with me. I don't

have the skills to make my shop successful without his help. He's even renovating my house—and for what? I won't even date him. For once, I just want someone to fix me. *Me!* Because I'm too messed up to figure it out on my own."

The sisters glanced at each other, then Megan spoke. "That's not true. You view all these problems as weaknesses, instead of seeing why Alex is doing all of this. He's doing it because he cares for you. Can't you see that?"

Lily rose and walked to her closet to avoid responding to Megan. Even if Alex cared, she could never return it, at least not in the same way.

As she looked at the black silk dress she was supposed to wear for the grand opening, she heard Cassidy's plea. "Lily? You don't need fixing. You are good enough to do this. And you're good enough for Alex."

She shook her head, afraid to turn around and face the truth.

Megan agreed. "Cass is right. Tonight, you need to act like you believe it." She heard her sisters' footsteps behind her, then they slowly wrapped their arms around her.

Even if she couldn't accept it, their belief made her feel like it was true. She was enough for Alex. For everything tonight would bring.

CHAPTER TWENTY-TWO

ALEX

Two weeks. That's all the time he had left before he'd head back to LA.

The fresh air during his morning run on the beach revived him as he dodged the tide, the sun stretching over him, his feet kicking up sand.

Something inside was still lingering over the dream of them together, living in her fixer-upper on the beach.

Never going to happen. Not when you have luck like mine. He almost muttered the thought aloud as he passed another beach home, where kids were building sandcastles in the morning light.

He had asked her to stay away, yet here he was, his thoughts preoccupied by her *again*. Why couldn't he just let her go and embrace his bachelor status? He could date whomever he wanted—nobody was tying him down. He had all the freedom in the world.

All the freedom. And none of the happiness.

His phone started ringing as Len's name popped up on the

screen. Recently, his agent had been emailing Alex about rene-
gotiating his contract since the show had been such a success.

"Hey, Len, what's up?"

"Good morning, Alex. It's your lucky day. You sitting down?"

"Not really. I'm on the beach taking my morning run." He
watched a line of sailboats making their way out of the harbor,
the wind pushing them along like toy boats.

"That works too. I talked with the studio this week.
They're willing to renegotiate your contract if they can
increase the number of episodes for next season. Your
schedule is going to be crazy, but they're going to pay you well
for it. I think you'll like what you'll see on the new contract.
You're going to be one of the highest paid stars on the
network."

Alex stopped on the beach, still breathing hard, watching
two seagulls fight over a scrap of bread.

"Really? That's great news." He couldn't wait to tell Lily. If he
was traveling more, maybe he could make it back to Wild
Harbor. Better yet, persuade her to meet up with him on one of
these trips. They could see New York together. Seattle. San
Francisco.

"I'll send the information later today. Look it over and let me
know what you think. Although, I'm not sure why you'd ever
want to turn this down."

Alex shifted his weight. "Yeah, you're right. Thanks, Len. I'll
be in touch." He hung up and looked across the lake. Life
seemed to have taken a promising turn.

My lucky day.

While he was staring at the sailboats on the horizon, two
older ladies approached, their faces glowing as the morning sun
caught their round cheeks.

"Are you Alex Briggs?" one of them asked, eyes wide.

He nodded.

"I'm Edna." Her white hair glinted in the light, as she turned to her friend. "This is Thelma." She pointed to her friend, who couldn't stop smiling.

"Alex, I love your show," said Thelma. "Especially your part. Now, if I was just thirty years younger—"

Alex thought thirty years probably wasn't enough, but he just smiled and nodded. Fans like these were taking the show to new heights.

"I love your show too," Edna said, not to be outdone by her friend. "We were hoping to see you at the big bash tonight and get your autograph. I'm going to be wearing my fan T-shirt."

"Oh, great." Alex tried to sound excited. "A fan shirt?"

Thelma spoke up, trying to beat Edna's response. "We both got T-shirts with a picture of your face on the front. We were hoping you could sign them."

Alex lifted his eyebrows and nodded slowly. He had no idea what to say. *His face on a T-shirt?*

"You might want to consider selling these shirts," Edna said. "I bet a lot of ladies would want one."

The women both smiled and nodded, their faces beaming with adoration.

This is awkward. "Thanks, I'll think about it," he replied, already deciding that he would *not* be selling T-shirts with his face plastered on the front. Even his mom wouldn't own a shirt like that. "I probably should go. Lots to do before tonight. See you at the event."

He backed away and gave them a quick wave, resuming his jog down the beach.

If the day was already starting out this well, he had a feeling that nothing could go wrong. He stopped in the sand for one last look at the cloudless blue sky over the water. The sailboats bobbed along, tiny blue dots in the distance.

For once, things were finally working out.

~

"How about if we put a shelf here? How would that look?"

Alex was staring out the window of Lily's home, barely aware Alli was talking.

"Hey, Alex, I'm asking you a question." Alli poked him on the shoulder.

"What? Oh, sorry, I got distracted."

"I can tell. I was suggesting where we put this white shelf. If we don't get this right, it will ruin the whole wall."

"Oh, right." He didn't sound convincing. He barely glanced at the wall. "Sure, whatever you think is best."

"Alex Briggs, are you even paying attention to me?"

"Uh-huh." He avoided looking at her. An idea sprang into his head about the house next door—a really crazy idea. But since his phone call with Len, he believed nothing could stop him.

He felt a tug on his arm. "What has you so preoccupied?"

He turned and looked at Alli. "I'm helping with the chocolate shop grand opening tonight. Doing Lily a favor."

She nodded. "I heard you've been spotted around town with her. Your picture from the concert made front page news." She crossed her arms and gave him a smile that hinted of jealousy.

"That's a small-town newspaper for you."

"Oh, hey, congrats on the news about the show."

"Did Len tell you? I haven't even signed the contract yet."

"Who else? I'm happy for you. Must be your dream come true."

"Yeah, I guess." He avoided her gaze. Even though he had been excited about his turn of luck, he had put the contract aside to sign later.

"What do you mean, you guess? Everyone loves you—what more could you want?"

He rubbed the sweat off his brow. The day had turned extremely warm, making the house stifling. "Do you ever wonder if it's worth it? All this traveling and sacrificing? Don't you ever just want to settle down some place?"

She made a face like she had bit into a lemon. "Not really." She narrowed her gaze. "You're not having second thoughts, are you? Because a lot of people are dependent on this show. Including me."

The way she was scrutinizing him made Alex shift uncomfortably. She was right. The entire crew was dependent on him. If he ever left, they'd all be out of work, scrambling to find a new gig. He had always known this was true, but now he felt the weight on his shoulders. It was one thing to have your show cancelled without a say, but it was another thing to back out and leave everyone stranded.

"I don't take my responsibility lightly."

"Well, good." She resumed her million-dollar smile. She took a step closer and touched his arm. Her voice dropped low as she leaned toward him, whispering in his ear. "I'm glad you can see reason for once. Now, if you could just give me a chance, you'd see what a powerhouse couple we'd be together."

He pulled away. "Alli, you know how I feel about *this*. Bad for the show. Plus, I'm not interested."

Her eyes flicked to the window.

As he turned to follow her gaze, he saw a passing shadow, then nothing.

He looked back at her. "I thought I saw something, but . . ."

He took one last look at the window. Probably his imagination.

She picked up a hammer and twirled it in her fingers. "I could tell the rest of the crew about you having second thoughts."

He put his hands in his pockets, weighing her words. "Why would you do that?"

"I don't know. Maybe it's time you do something nice for me."

"Something nice?" He shook his head. "You want to blackmail me? Never thought you'd stoop that low."

"I wouldn't call it that. It's just business as usual in Hollywood." She smiled coyly.

Alex frowned, pushing back the pulsing anger. He took a step farther away. "It's not the way I do business, Alli."

"You're not going to answer me? Listen, Alex Briggs, I've given everything to this show. *Everything.* And I won't let you throw it away. Don't you care about your future? If you walk out on us now, you'll never work in Hollywood again."

He turned and walked out of the home, slamming the door behind him.

No way would he bend to blackmail. He'd sign the contract and return it to Len as soon as possible, so Alli wouldn't have any grounds to accuse him. It would lock him in for at least a year. But with her threats, it was the only option now.

CHAPTER TWENTY-THREE

LILY

"I really don't like this idea." Lily closed her eyes as her sisters led her into the chocolate shop. "If I trip and fall down, I'm going to blame you both."

They had insisted she walk into her store without peeking so they could surprise her with the decorations.

"We're almost there," Cassidy said, the excitement barely contained in her voice. "Open your eyes on the count of three."

Together they counted: "One, two, three!"

Lily opened her eyes and stared at the transformation. All the tables in the shop were decked in red roses, pink dahlias, and an array of baby's breath and greenery. An archway, draped in trailing vines and more flowers, was centered in the room. Chocolates were stacked on tiered trays on the counter, lined with more flowers and illuminated by tiny candles. The shop's pendant lights were dimmed, while floating candles twinkled on every shelf in the room.

She raised her hands to her lips, trying to stop herself from crying. "It's beautiful. More than I could have dreamed of."

"Don't you dare cry!" Megan teased. "You just put your makeup on. We can't have mascara streaming down your face, giving you raccoon eyes."

"Now, you're making me cry." Cassidy wiped her eyes.

"I refuse to get emotional about party decorations." Megan bit her lip. She was always the last of the sisters to show emotion, as if this somehow made her stronger.

Lily knew better.

Cassidy took Lily's hand. "You look so beautiful tonight. You might attract more attention than Alex."

Lily raised her eyebrows. "Not if Thelma and Edna can help it. I think they invited their entire bridge club."

Lily hoped the form-fitting silk sheath was not too showy. She wanted to look elegant and professional, not like she was trying *too* hard. She pulled at the dress to make it stop hugging her hips. "Are you sure it isn't too much? I don't want people to think—"

"That you're beautiful?" Megan smiled. "Lily, why are you always trying to hide who you are? You need stop overthinking things."

The door opened behind her, and she turned around to discover Alex dressed like she had never seen him before. Instead of wearing his usual faded jeans and T-shirt, he was decked out in a custom-tailored suit that had probably cost more than her entire wardrobe. She had never seen him look so handsome. She had to stop herself from staring.

Megan joined Alex. "Don't you clean up well? Guess I've never seen the Hollywood side of you before."

"Uh, thanks . . . I think? I don't dress up much. I'm more comfortable in a T-shirt than a suit." He paused and looked at Lily, his gaze sweeping over her dress. "Lily, you look stunning."

The heat in her face matched the roses in the room. "Thank you," she whispered.

A smirk on Megan's face warned her to stop tugging on the dress again.

Cassidy turned to Lily. "Wow, don't you think Alex is going to make all the girls swoon tonight?"

Alex chuckled, shaking his head, "More like all the senior ladies. I met two on the beach today who will be wearing fan T-shirts."

Lily laughed. She had a feeling Edna and Thelma were the culprits. Thelma had mentioned something about a special treat for Alex. "I wouldn't be surprised if they forced you to take a picture with them. But despite their faults, they're my most faithful customers, so please be on your best behavior."

"I will." He winked at her, and his eyes drifted to her hair.

She had pinned up one side, while the other hung in loose curls across her shoulder.

"I've never seen your hair that way. It looks nice."

"Oh, thanks. Cassidy talked me into wearing it this way." She ran her hand across her hair, suddenly feeling self-conscious as Alex studied her.

"Not to cut in, but we both have to run home and dress for the grand opening." Megan nodded to her sister that it was time to go. "We'll leave you two alone." She gave Lily a quick wink before heading out the door with Cassidy.

"So," Alex said filling the silence. "It's the big night. You ready for this?"

"As ready as I'll ever be. Thanks to you."

"Everything looks amazing, including you."

She looked down, afraid to respond. Why was she still so nervous to accept his kindness? "Alex, I can't thank you enough for what you've done—"

He looked at her, an intensity in his eyes. "I wanted to do it for you."

She shook her head. "I don't even deserve it."

"That's not true." He grabbed her hand.

The warmth of his grasp sent a shiver up her arm.

"You do deserve it. You need to let yourself accept it."

The bell on the door rang, interrupting their moment together. Lily looked over Alex's shoulder to see Ms. Patty, the town librarian, entering the shop. She reluctantly dropped Alex's hand. "We have company. She probably wants to get an early autograph from you. I'd bet money on it."

"Before you go—" Alex lowered his voice and drew closer to her. "I know you'll be busy tonight, but I wanted to talk to you afterward. Just the two of us."

Lily's heart rate quickened. "What is it?"

"Nothing to worry about. Just go and take care of your first guest. We'll talk later."

"Can't you even give me a hint?"

"Nice try."

She opened the door with a smile and greeting for Ms. Patty, but her mind already was racing ahead to the end of the evening.

~

THE EVENT WAS BETTER than Lily could have dreamed.

Most of Wild Harbor showed up, with a line streaming out the door and another forming for Alex, who turned out to be one of the biggest draws for the event.

Every guest who talked with Alex received his full attention, letting them take selfies and signing autographs. Lily smiled as Alex greeted people by name, from cute preschoolers to one-hundred-and-three-year-old Hazel Van Strutton, who was wheelchair bound.

All night, Lily sneaked glances at Alex, who occasionally caught her eye and gave her a quick wink. Even when Thelma and Edna came in with their matching T-shirts, proudly presenting Alex's face, he played along, never revealing his true feelings. He offered to sign both shirts, which made Thelma and Edna giggle with delight.

Lily would probably never hear the end of it.

If they ever find out I've kissed Alex, they will never let me live it down. Lily smiled at the thought. She had liked kissing Alex.

Maybe too much.

During the event, Megan managed crowd control, while Cassidy and Matt were flooded with buyers wanting boxes of gourmet chocolates, truffles, and blocks of fudge. Lily chatted with guests and took orders for future events, including three graduation parties, two baby showers, and a family reunion. She needed three months of chocolate orders to pay the bills for another quarter and give her some breathing room.

If tonight was a success, she had Alex to thank.

Megan tapped Lily on the shoulder. "The mayor wants a picture."

"What?" Lily spotted the mayor chatting with Alex. "He probably wants a celebrity shot with Alex. Not me."

"This is no time to be a wallflower." Megan took Lily's arm and escorted her toward the men. "After all, you're the owner. This is good advertising."

"But—" Lily tried to protest, but her sister shoved her gently toward Alex, who looked up just as she approached.

"I want a picture for *The Wild Harbor News.*" Megan pulled out her cell phone.

Alex wrapped his right arm around Lily's waist while the mayor stood on the other side.

She had to admit that feeling his arm wrapped around her waist made her heart race as she felt the warmth of his hand pressing against her. An obligatory gesture for the picture, but she noticed that he let his palm linger afterward, until Lily was called away by another guest.

CHAPTER TWENTY-FOUR

LILY

By the time the event ended, Lily's ankle ached from standing all evening. Tossing her high heels aside, she padded across the wood floor in bare feet, gathering all the bouquets, ready to change out of her dress. She'd take the flowers to the hospital tomorrow to donate to patients.

Alex joined the cleanup efforts, taking off his coat and rolling up his shirtsleeves to wash trays. Lily couldn't help but notice how good his muscular arms looked when wet.

Cassidy piped up from the iPad they used for sales. "This is unbelievable." She stared in wonder at the sales report. "Lily, come see this. You sold out of four kinds of chocolate, and there's barely any fudge left."

Lily set down the punch bowl and made a beeline for the screen. She touched it with her finger. "What? That's impossible. I made three months worth of chocolate. There's no way we're sold out. Did you check the refrigerator in back?"

Cassidy nodded. "Totally wiped out. The report here proves it. You know what that means, right? You won't have to close the shop. You have enough to get through summer and maybe even hire some help."

Lily stared open-mouthed at the report. "I don't know what to say. I can't wrap my mind around it."

Matt replied from across the room as he swept the floor. "Then don't say anything. Just let yourself celebrate, for once."

Her brother knew her well. Ever the optimist, they were opposites in a lot of ways. He knew that she would already be fretting about how she could afford to pay for help. But like it or not, her brother was right. She needed to celebrate this win. Her shop had turned a profit. As long as it grew, she'd be able to fulfill her dream of establishing a lifelong career here.

Alex was drying his hands on a towel. "Your brother's right this time." He smiled at her. "A celebration is in order."

"Anyone want to head to Brewster's? I'm starving." Matt stacked trays.

"Sure," Megan replied. "Let's get carryout. You are welcome to come to my place."

Lily sank onto a nearby stool. "I'd love to guys, but I can't. My ankle hurts. Sorry to bail, but go on without me."

"Are you sure?" Cassidy said.

Lily nodded and gave her sister a hug. "You've done enough for me tonight. Go have fun."

Alex put the towel down and walked toward Lily and her sister. "How about I take Lily home, and you guys can head out? We're almost done here anyway."

With the excitement of the night, Lily had forgotten about going to Alex's rental afterward. She took a deep breath, trying to settle her mixed emotions about being alone with him.

"Let me put away this box, and we can head out." She picked up the box and carried it away from Alex.

As she walked to the storage room, Matt followed her. "Hey, Lily, I've been wanting to talk to you about something, but I didn't want to ruin your grand opening."

"You can't possibly ruin tonight."

"Well, I wasn't sure you'd want to know because it's about Alex."

She turned toward him. "Okay, what is it?"

He shifted uncomfortably and dropped his voice. "Today, when I ran back to your house to grab an extra broom from your garage, I accidentally saw something." He glanced behind him to make sure no one was there. "I'm only telling you this because I'm your brother and want to protect you."

"Matt, just tell me."

"Well, when I walked by the window, Alex was with that girl from the show."

"Alli? He's with her quite a bit. It's his job."

"I know." He paused. "But . . ."

"Just say it."

"They were standing close together—she was touching his arm, whispering in his ear. It just didn't seem like a working relationship, if you know what I mean."

Lily shook her head and looked at the floor, unable to make sense of what Matt was suggesting. "He has no interest in her. He told me so."

"I'm just telling you what I saw."

She closed her eyes. The swift sting of betrayal pricked her. She had trusted Alex to be totally honest. Hadn't he just confessed his feelings for her? She didn't understand.

Matt regarded her with concern. "Maybe I shouldn't have told you."

"No." She held up her hand. "I'm glad you did. It's not like we are in a relationship. I thought it best if we weren't dating. Now, I know why."

Matt touched her arm before he left. "Call me if you need anything."

She wanted to be angry with Matt, but she couldn't. He was saving her from more pain.

Lily joined her siblings and tried to pretend her world hadn't just been shaken.

"I think we're done for the night." Cassidy set down the last box of supplies on the counter next to the display case. "How are you still standing?"

"I'm not sure." Lily rubbed her ankle. "I'll probably collapse as soon as I get home." She felt the truth of that statement in more ways than one.

"Anything I can do to help?"

Lily shook her head and waved to her siblings as they headed out the door.

An hour ago, she couldn't wait to be alone with Alex. Now, her head ached at the thought of facing him.

As ALEX slowly drove through town, the streetlights illuminated the outline of his chiseled face. The whole evening had been colored by the news about Alli.

Why was she always falling for men who wounded her so deeply? If only she didn't love him so much it hurt.

There, I said it.

It had always been love. She just hadn't wanted to admit it.

When they pulled into the driveway at his rental, Alex hopped out and circled around the truck to help her. "No reason to make your ankle hurt worse than it already does." He opened her door and held his hand out.

"Put your arm around my shoulder and use me as your crutch," he said, wrapping his hand around her waist.

His arm, tucked securely around her, felt like a natural fit. Yet the ache of betrayal sparked anger in her heart.

How can I both want him and loathe him at the same time?

"Let me try to walk." She pulled away from him and tried to step with her sore ankle again. Pain shot up her leg. She didn't want his help, but she didn't have a choice. The constant standing all evening had been too much for her weak ankle. Reluctantly, she wrapped her arm around his shoulder as they walked around the back of the house where she could put her foot up in a chair.

After she sat, she leaned back with a deep sigh, relieved to have some space. "This is better."

"Can I get you a drink? I have water, soda, or milk."

She let out a laugh. "Milk? Do you entertain a lot of four-year-olds?"

"I didn't want to hold back any options. Plus I've known a few guys who love a glass of cold milk. Myself included."

"Mmm. Tempting, but I'll take water."

"Coming right up, for the star of the evening." He left her alone for a few minutes to fetch her drink.

She listened to the sound of waves crashing somewhere in the darkness.

It was true she could get used to this. To be his. Someone she could trust her whole heart with. She wanted so badly to trust again, and she wanted it to be him.

Alex came through the door carrying drinks. He had shed his suit coat and rolled up the sleeves of his dress shirt, looking more like the Alex she remembered.

As he cracked open a diet soda and settled in the Adirondack chair next to hers, he looked at her with a proud grin on his face. "So, tonight was a win, right?"

"Yes, in most ways." She averted her eyes, avoiding his gaze that seemed to penetrate her thoughts.

"Well, I thought so." He tilted his head. "The event was incredible. You were stunning. Perfect on the red carpet in that dress."

Was this just his usual line to women?

She was glad for the darkness, which masked her reaction. "What did you want to tell me?"

"Len, my agent, called today. Not only is my contract going to be renewed, but they want me to travel even more this year. The show's ratings have been good, and they want even more episodes." He paused, waiting for her reaction.

She sat up straighter, turning toward him. "That's great, Alex. I'm happy for you."

Her problem was being solved after all. Alex was leaving.

The lines between his eyebrows deepened as he stared at her. "That's funny, because you don't look happy."

She turned away. "This is your dream, right? Everything you wanted."

"Not everything." He paused, took a breath. "Not you."

"I can still be your friend."

"I want more than that."

"Face it. I'm not your type." She waved her hand in the air. "I'm just the girl next door. The little sister you never had."

"I may have seen you that way at one time. But not in high school—and definitely not now. I love spending time with you."

"Along with every other girl."

He frowned. "What are you talking about?"

"My brother saw you with Alli."

His eyes widened. "You mean at your house today?" He put his hands up in defense. "It wasn't like it appeared."

"How can you say that?"

"Because Alli isn't the person I dream about. The one I can't get out of my head. Lily, my every thought has been fixed on you ever since I came back. You're the one I want."

She rubbed her hand across her throbbing forehead. She couldn't let herself believe him. She'd been burned before. "But you're leaving. You got a new contract."

"I don't want a new contract if I can't have you." He leaned toward her, his face meeting hers. He reached for her hands. "Lily, I didn't think I'd feel this way. But it helped me to realize —a life of fame isn't really what I want. I want to settle down, get married, raise a family. And I want that with you. I just don't know how to convince you of that."

She shook her head. "You can't just quit the show."

"I can, and I will."

"This is a chance of a lifetime."

"It is. I'd like to give them one more year—if you'll wait. But if I have to choose you or them, I'll choose you."

"You'd be crazy not to take this opportunity. Alex, this is your dream."

"Then come with me." He took her hands in his. "You can meet me in different cities."

"What? No! You're being ridiculous." She shook her head and pulled her hands away. "Everything in my life is here. I can't just leave Wild Harbor. You need to go on this tour."

"At least, agree to wait for me. I'll come back to Wild Harbor whenever I have a break. Let me give it one more year before I leave the show for good."

"Alex, how could that work? I'm tied to the chocolate shop. Mom and Dad need help. I can't just run off any time I want to. I don't care what you say, our lives are on completely different paths."

"Then I'll quit."

"I can't let you do this. You won't throw away your career for me. Don't you understand?" She tried to stand but her ankle was too sore, causing her to stumble back into her chair.

Alex reached to steady her, grabbing her arm. As he caught her, she covered her face so he wouldn't see the pain he was causing. "I can't be with you Alex. Please. I can't talk about this anymore. I just need to go home."

Alex stood still, his jaw set. He started to say something, then looked at the ground. "If that's what you want then—"

That's not what I want. I want you, she wanted to confess, but she would not say anything more.

The crashing waves were breaking inside her. One after

another. Pulling her under, drowning her. She would not let him see her pain. Instead, she would silently release him, letting go of any chance to change the ending to their story.

"It's the only way," she whispered.

She wanted to take her words back. To make right what she had broken. But she couldn't breathe. The air had been taken from her lungs, stolen as quickly as her last hope.

CHAPTER TWENTY-FIVE

ALEX

A week went by without seeing her. Every morning when he woke, his first thought was Lily. But instead of feeling hopeful, the distance between them left him with the slow, dull ache of emptiness. He still had one more week until he'd be finished with her home and then leaving Wild Harbor. *Gotta get used to this,* he told himself as he dragged himself out of bed. *Pull the bandage off quick.*

When he picked up his jeans, a coin fell out and rolled across the floor, catching the sunlight. It reminded him of his lucky silver dollar from his grandfather, the one he'd lost in the lake when he was seven. When it had slipped from his hand, he had lunged at it, fervently trying to grab it. The more he tried, though, the more the waters churned, pushing away the coin into the black abyss. He had swum around, straining his eyes under the murky waters, wrapped in cold darkness. But the coin had slipped from his fingers and disappeared for good, buried in the bottomless sand. Every day he had searched the shore for it. Every day he had come home empty-handed.

"Forget the coin. There will be others," his mom had told him.

But Alex still thought of that coin, so long gone, and how there was nothing he could do. Now, the memory seemed like a joke. Who cared about a stupid coin when he was losing everything?

Grief had a way of putting his whole life into perspective. The more he reached for what he had lost, the more it was driven away into the murky void, beyond where he could see.

He couldn't stop thinking about the night when Lily had pushed him away for good. After their argument, he had driven Lily to her parent's home in horrible silence, realizing he was losing her just like before.

"It's for the best," she had said as she exited the car, looking at him with an expression he couldn't read, her jaw set, her eyes hard.

There was so much he could have said to her, so much complicated past to sort through. He could have pleaded. Begged. Fought for her.

Instead, all he could do was silently nod.

She'd slammed the door and slipped into her parent's home. Gone for good, like the coin in the water.

WHEN HE ARRIVED AT WORK, Mike approached, sipping a cup of coffee from his thermos. "You okay? You look terrible."

Alex pulled a ladder out of his truck. "Couldn't sleep."

"Let me guess. Girlfriend problems?"

"Don't ask. I do not want to talk about it."

"You're mister cheerful this morning. Not to be the bearer of bad news, but Jeb is sick today, and one of the crew broke the antique mirror in Lily's home."

"You're kidding. Why couldn't it at least have been something easy to replace?"

"I thought the same thing. Not that it could be helped. But if Lily's already mad at you, this isn't going to make things better."

"I'll find something." Alex shouldered the ladder. "You said Jeb is sick too?"

"Yep. The flu. He was supposed to patch that spot on Lily's roof, where it was leaking. Everyone is stressed about the timeline for finishing things. I can try to work on it, but I need to pick up supplies this morning, and I have a million things on my list to get done."

"I'll climb on the roof and do it. Then I'll head to the salvage shop and see if they have a mirror. Knowing my luck, he won't have anything even close to the same. But it's worth a try."

Alex carried the extension ladder to the house and scaled it to the roof, distracted by the unexpected repairs adding up. As he stood on top of the ladder and looked for the leak, he stepped forward onto the roof and slipped on some loose shingle granules. Losing his balance, he tried to step back to regain his footing, only to aim too close to the edge of the roof, where his foot slipped off. The surface of the roof fell away as he tumbled through the air and onto the grass. He landed on his back with a loud *oof,* whacking the back of his head in the process. He closed his eyes as the world spun around him.

Guess this is what it feels like to hit rock bottom.

He clenched his teeth, reeling from the stabbing sensation in his head.

He heard Mike's voice in the distance. "Are you okay?"

Alex winced and grabbed the back of his head. "I think so, but that's going to hurt tomorrow. I'm just glad it's a one-story." Alex slowly sat up. His back wrenched in pain. "Forget what I said about tomorrow. It hurts *now.*"

"Uh, maybe you should stay on the ground for a minute," Mike said. "I'll have one of the guys get you some ice."

As Alex lay on the ground, icing his head and back, he studied the maple tree shading him. He tried praying, even though it felt like he was ranting to himself more than actually conversing with God. For once, he had to get it out.

Maybe this is all a big joke. Some lesson I'm supposed to learn, but I don't understand. I'm trying so hard for Lily, and for what? To be shut out of her life for good? Why did you have me come here if it was only to get hurt?

Alex didn't know what to expect, but he received no response. Just the crash of waves in the distance and the slow ache of waiting for an answer.

WHEN THE PAINKILLERS finally kicked in, Alex ambled to his truck and hauled his sore body into the driver's seat. He didn't want to see Joshua today. Didn't want to listen to his puzzling advice. But the mirror was broken, and Joshua was the only one in town who might have something to replace it.

At the salvage shop, Joshua bent over a glass trinket, his glasses perched on the end of his nose. Without looking up he said, "I wondered when you'd be in."

Alex caught a glimpse of the trinket more clearly. *Another bird.*

What was this guy's thing with birds? First, the window. Now this.

"How'd you know?" Alex asked.

"You're working on an old house." He glanced over the top of his glasses. "Things always go wrong."

"It's a little late for that advice. I should have chosen a different house."

"It's no coincidence that the only two homes on the beach that needed to be fixed up were right next to each other. Perfect for two families who need each other."

"We're selling the one next to Lily's. She's staying put. I doubt she'll know the family that buys the one next door."

"Perhaps. Take a seat. Looks like you need it." Joshua nodded toward a wooden stool nearby, then turned his attention back to his work. Engrossed in fixing the bird, Joshua sat as he examined the figurine. "Have you had time to make it to the cemetery yet?"

Alex shook his head. "Don't see the point of it."

More like, he *avoided* it. He didn't want to be reminded of his dad or anything unpleasant from his past. "It's not like he's there."

"It's not for your dad," the old man said, an unreadable look in his eyes. "It's for you."

"Not sure I know what you mean." Alex watched Joshua's nimble fingers place the bird's wing delicately on the figurine. He wasn't sure why the object was worth fixing. It didn't look particularly valuable.

But what did he know? He only found worth in things that seemed useful and served a function—tools, doors, handles. A bird trinket seemed like nothing more than a piece from a glass menagerie. Worthless. Broken.

"Not to interrupt you, but I've got a problem," Alex said.

"Most people do."

"A broken mirror in Lily's home. I need to find something to replace it. You got anything like that?"

Joshua stood, his eyes sparkling. "I have mirrors. But that's not your problem. Least not the one you really need solved. But follow me."

He walked to a side room, where picture frames were stacked on the floor. To the left were mirrors, in various sizes, lined up on the floor and hanging on the wall. Oblong and rectangular. Ovals and squares, ornately cut, in every shape and size. Yellowed with time, once capturing hundreds of faces.

Now, they only reflected a dingy room of castaways. A hall of mirrors reflecting the past.

"I've got some beauties," Joshua said, his reflection duplicated across a dozen mirrors. "Just need to see past the flaws. Some might have a small chip in the edge or the frame is broken. Because of age, the reflection isn't as clear. But no less beautiful."

Alex knelt and examined a mirror on the floor.

"It makes me think of the verse, 'For now we see only a reflection as in a mirror; then we shall see face to face,'" Joshua recited. "Someday, we will understand things so much more clearly than we do now."

Joshua studied the bird in his hands. "Do you know why I'm fixing this?" He held up the bird in a shaft of light as mirrors reflected a dozen birds back.

Alex shook his head.

"Because most people only see it as a broken object." He lifted the cut glass figurine so it sparkled, sending light spinning into the room. Suddenly, the dingy room seemed to glow, brilliantly lit by sunlight on glass, reflected back in every mirror. "But there is always more we cannot see."

"You have a way with seeing things, Joshua." Alex squinted in the dazzling light. He turned and found a rectangular mirror framed in an ornate gold frame. It was dirty, yellowed with age.

"Before something can be restored, you have to imagine what it *could be*. You have to see *past* the brokenness. True for birds . . ." He paused, looked at the glass figure, then at Alex. "And people."

He held Alex's gaze for a moment before Alex looked away.

"Some things can't be fixed," Alex said quietly.

"In this life, yes. But not forever." He placed the figurine on a shelf nearby and nodded toward the mirror. "If you can see past the flaws, that one will shine up real nice."

"What do I owe you for it?"

"Just take it and use it. That's all I ask."

"You let me have the window for free too. I need to pay you something."

"Consider it a gift." Joshua returned to his worktable in the middle of the shop, surrounded by more broken figurines.

"I don't know how to thank you." Alex picked up the mirror.

"You don't have to." Joshua smiled.

Alex carried the mirror from the salvage shop, shaking his head as he lifted it into the truck. He wasn't about to change his mind about leaving Wild Harbor, but as Alex drove back to Lily's house, he abruptly turned toward the cemetery, headed a mile up the road, and pulled into a long drive.

His father's grave was located on the grassy hill ahead. He parked along the side of the drive and walked toward it, his feet kicking stones on the road. Reading the passing grave-stones, he noticed couples who had been married fifty years or more, their lives summed up in a few words etched in stone.

What were their stories? Did anyone speak their names? What would they do if they had more time?

It suddenly hit him where he had heard the verse Joshua had recited as he looked in the mirror. Alex had read it at his dad's funeral, in front of a crowded congregation packed into an old church with creaky wood floors and polished pews.

When he finished and took his seat next to his mother, the only close family member he had left, he had wanted to say so much more to the people of Wild Harbor. He had wanted to tell them his dad wasn't just a man whose life had been taken by cancer. He was a father who had dedicated long hours to building things with his hands, then had returned home and used those same calloused hands to play catch with Alex or to dance in the kitchen with Mom while the radio played.

He had made a life for them, a beautiful life filled with color and sound and laughter and love. Alex knew that his dad had embodied that love, had breathed it like air, and it had filled everyone around him.

How unfair it had seemed to Alex that his life had been taken so soon, when everyone else's parents still lived. If only Alex had known his father's time on earth was going to be cut short. He had counted on more time.

Then when his mom had announced she was remarrying, Alex had felt the sting of losing her too, the gradual falling apart of his history, like a seam slowly unraveling. He hadn't known those he loved would slip from his fingers. He hadn't accumulated enough people in his life to offset the ones he'd lost. He'd thought they would always be together, his dad and mom still swaying gently in the kitchen to the radio.

Alex took the path toward his father's grave, the place where all his dreams had broken, where his future had tilted and shifted toward an unknown path. He had thought fame would fill that void. But now that he had achieved his so-called success, he realized it was meaningless.

When he'd left Wild Harbor at twenty-two, moving away was the one thing he had sought to rid himself of his pain. Now, distance was the wedge that had driven him and Lily apart.

He didn't know why he had come to the cemetery or what he was looking for. All he wanted now was for someone to reverse time and piece together all the broken things again, just like Joshua had done with the bird.

He knelt and traced his father's name on the stone with his finger.

His father's life work, encapsulated in a few words. Whatever dreams he had longed for were cut short. *What would you do if you had more time?*

He would never know his dad's answer. But he knew Dad's story was part of his own story. And his story was not over yet.

For the first time in a long time, Alex experienced the rush of something breaking open inside as the tears began to fall.

The walls that had hidden his grief were finally disintegrating, falling, tumbling down. Instead of feeling pain, he experienced what he could describe as relief. Freedom. *Letting go.*

Like the birds in the stained glass. Finally flying away from what had bound him for so long.

CHAPTER TWENTY-SIX

LILY

"You've barely eaten a thing for breakfast. This is your big day. You should at least eat something." Her mom was scrutinizing Lily's full plate of scrambled eggs as they gathered around the oak dining room table. Mom gave the same look of concern as when Lily was little.

But this time, Lily's lack of an appetite had nothing to do with the food.

"I'm nervous, that's all."

"Oh, sweetheart, I know. All they want is for you to be yourself on camera. You'll be wonderful."

Lily didn't want to tell her mom the truth—that it wasn't just the home reveal day putting her emotions in turmoil, but seeing Alex again after two weeks. After she broke things off, the text messages and visits had stopped. Not that she could blame him. When she had asked him to let her go, he had dropped out of her life as quickly as he had appeared in it, confirming everything she had feared.

I don't deserve a guy like Alex.

LOVE AT WILD HARBOR

She had spent the last two weeks burying herself in work, making and eating more chocolates than needed, trying to take her mind off him. But it wasn't working. All she could think about was what his arms had felt like around her. When she was at her parent's house, she cried and moped, trying to hide her emotions so her family wouldn't suspect anything was wrong.

But her mother had noticed something was off and gave her a concerned look. "Are you okay?"

"I'm fine, Mom."

"You don't seem fine. Is it because Alex is leaving soon? You two have spent a lot of time together since he's been home."

"No," she said quickly.

Her mom sighed.

"Okay, maybe. We had a falling out the night of the grand opening. We haven't talked since."

"I wondered. The ladies in the book club have been asking me what's going on between you two. Diane Sutton said she saw you together. She's been asking for updates, and I told her I was trying to respect your privacy. But I couldn't help but notice lately that you seemed down—and that Alex hasn't come calling."

"I asked him not to see me."

"But why?" Mom sat next to her. "Is there something he's done?"

She shook her head.

Quite the opposite.

"He's been nothing but good to me. The problem is . . . I can't see a future with him. He's not staying in Wild Harbor, and I'm not leaving here. There's no way it would ever work."

"But how do you know? Have you given him a chance?"

"He found out they want him to do even more episodes this year. He'll be traveling the country constantly. He doesn't have time for a relationship."

"Did he tell you that?"

185

"No, not exactly. He told me he'd quit the show."

"Well, then. There's your answer. He's giving up something important for something even more important. You."

"I'm not going to be the reason he quits the show. I can't do that to him. He would resent me the rest of his life for taking away the one thing he's always wanted."

"Are you sure that's what he really wants? Sometimes, people change. You need to give him a chance."

"I gave him a chance—in high school. By the time he changed his mind, it was too late."

"Do you remember when you were a little girl and were always trying on my wedding dress? Some moms don't let their kids touch their wedding dress. They box it up and hide it away on a high shelf, like some sort of sacred object. They're afraid of getting it dirty, but I didn't worry about that with you girls. That's because there was a time I didn't think I'd marry at all."

"What? You never told me that. I thought it was love at first sight with Dad."

"Your dad says that. But it wasn't for me. When I met your dad, I'd just had my heart broken after senior prom. I was waitressing at the Bluebird restaurant, and he came in. I thought he was handsome, but I wasn't ready to date again." Becky plucked a flower from the vase on the table before going on.

"He just kept coming in and talking to me. Then one day, he asked me out. I told him I couldn't date him, but I was too embarrassed to say it wasn't because of anything he did—I was afraid of getting hurt. So, Bill stopped coming in. I missed seeing his face, but my pride refused to let me admit it." Becky twirled the flower in her fingers, the petals spinning like a pinwheel.

"Then my friend, Diane, set me straight, saying, 'If you don't tell him how you feel, some other girl will snatch him up in a heartbeat. Bill is a good man, and he won't be single for long.'

"That's all I needed to hear. I raced down to his parents'

house and knocked on his door. When he opened it, I said, 'Bill, I miss seeing you at the restaurant and I don't want to go another day without telling you I'm sorry I ever turned you down for a date.' He just smiled and then asked, 'Well, how about now?' He never held it against me, not in more than thirty years of being married. I never regretted going back to him. Not once."

"Mom, you never told me the full story. I can't believe you asked Dad out."

"It wasn't the conventional thing to do, that's for sure. But your father never told anyone. Not even my mother, who would not have approved of a girl asking a boy."

"But things were different for you two—you were meant to be together."

"I didn't know that at the time. And neither do you." She placed the flower gently behind Lily's ear.

Lily looked down at her untouched plate of food. She had burned bridges with Alex for good. "I'm not sure it will make any difference now."

Her mom placed a hand on Lily's. "Honey, will you at least try to enjoy yourself today? Even if nothing is resolved between you and Alex, don't let it ruin your big day."

"I'll try." Lily carried her plate to the sink. She wasn't even sure Alex would talk to her.

She had replayed their moment in the garden when he had kissed her, his hands on her back, the warmth of his body next to hers. It was everything she had dreamed about, but the brokenness from her past with Thomas had left her wounded. Why had she fallen for Alex, a man she could never have? Why couldn't have he turned out to be a jerk, so he'd be easy to let go of?

Her mom joined her in the kitchen. "Let me do the dishes. You get ready for the big day."

"I have a couple hours before he wants me to arrive." She

glanced at her watch. "I need to stop at the shop to pick up chocolates for the cast and crew, then I'll meet you at my house."

"Oh, by the way, Alex told me he has a few surprises up his sleeve today."

Lily took the flower from her ear and grabbed her car keys. "Just what I need—more of the unexpected."

"Lily, sometimes the unexpected *is* just what we need. You know, it's never truly unexpected." She lifted her eyebrows, suggesting something more.

"Well, if you're talking about God, then I wish He'd tell me what I should do about Alex. I could use a little divine guidance right now."

She walked out the door, counting how many chocolates she'd need after filming today's finale. She didn't have time for the unexpected today. More than ever, she just wanted to get this day over with.

CHAPTER TWENTY-SEVEN

LILY

A s Lily reached to unlock the back door to her shop, she realized it had been left open.

"Not again." Most likely, one of her siblings had come in and forgotten to lock it. Ever since the break-in, she had made sure to take the cash with her. Unless someone wanted chocolate, they weren't going to find much to steal in her shop.

Lily's mind shifted back to what she needed to pick up. She entered and flipped on a single hall light, enough to see her way to the back storage room, where she kept the boxes of chocolates refrigerated. She walked into the darkened room and started pulling chocolates from the fridge, stacking them on top of the deep freezer.

When she heard a footstep behind her, something went cold in her body, an instinct of danger pulsing through her. She turned quickly.

A figure stood nearby, the whites of his eyes glaring in the darkness, a face she knew all too well.

"Thomas, what are you doing here?" Her voice was almost breathless as she tried to steady it so he couldn't hear her fear.

"Waiting for you."

"But why—"

"Why won't you return my text messages?" Thomas was blocking the door, the only way out of the back room.

She shifted her weight uncomfortably, searching for a way she could call for help. Why had she insisted on making this last-minute stop?

She had at least an hour until she was supposed to arrive at the house, and the only person she had told about coming here was her mom.

Panic started to rise up in her. The last place she wanted to be was alone with Thomas in a shop that was closed for the day. She needed out of here.

"Why don't we go somewhere to talk? We could head over to the coffee shop for something to drink—"

"No," he said quickly. "We can talk right here."

Lily's body stiffened. He wasn't giving her options. "Okay, can we at least go out front and sit at a table?" Anything that would give her visibility instead of being stuck in a windowless back room, where no one could see or hear her.

"No, I said *right here.*"

She swallowed hard.

The irritation was starting to grow in his voice.

She nodded and glanced around the room. What would get her out of this situation? Her phone was in her back jeans pocket, useless unless she could find a way to distract him. Lily was suddenly angry with herself for not thinking through how she would protect herself after the break-in.

"So, what is it you want to talk about?" She shifted again, trying to appear comfortable.

"I want to know what's going on between you and that guy."

"What guy? Are you talking about Alex? Nothing. He's leaving town this week."

"Nothing? Is that why I see pictures of you and him all over the Internet?"

"We went out on a few dates, but his show is ending today, then he's leaving Wild Harbor for good. You can ask him yourself." She pulled her phone from her pocket and held it out for him.

He shook his head.

She went on, trying to convince him. "I'm not making this up. Call him. Or I can."

He thought, then gave a quick nod. "I have a better idea. You call him and say you don't want him to ever contact you again. That things are over for good. Don't say anything about me. Just tell him what I said to you."

Her heartbeat thundered in her chest. "If I do that, you'll leave me alone?"

"Yeah. That's all I want—to hear that things are over between you two. For good."

"Okay. I'll do it. Just let me leave."

"Put it on speakerphone so I can hear."

She called Alex.

He picked up right away. She hadn't talked to him since their falling out, and his voice sounded gentle, almost apologetic.

"Hey, Lily. How are you?"

She tried to steady her voice, so she sounded calm, emotionless. "I'm fine. And you?"

Don't let him suspect anything and you can go home.

"I'm okay. I've missed talking to you."

Me too. She took a shaky breath. "Okay, so I need to get right to the point. I know I'll see you later today, but this can't wait. I have to tell you now." Her voice cracked a little from the tension. "I'm down at the shop right now. And I—" She stopped to take another breath but her thoughts seemed scattered, frightened.

What am I supposed to say?

She looked at Thomas, who mouthed some words: "Tell him it's over."

"I want to say—" she paused. It pained her to say these words, but she had no choice. "It's over between us."

Then Thomas whispered more words: "You never want to see him again."

"I—I can't see you again," she repeated flatly.

"But what about today? We have the home reveal—"

She repeated, "I can't—I can't see you."

"That he should never contact you again." Thomas crossed his arms.

"Please, don't contact me anymore." Her words were heartless.

For a moment, she couldn't hear anything on the other end. Time seemed frozen.

"Lily, what's going on?" Alex asked, an edge to his voice. "You agreed to complete the show. Whether or not you want to see me, I need you here today."

"Nothing is going on." She blinked back tears. "I'm here. Alone at the shop. In the back room. Talking to you." *Oh, how she wished he was here with her.*

If only he could see her, he'd know she didn't mean any of it. She hated that her words sounded so cold.

Alex paused. "You don't sound like yourself."

"End the call." Thomas whispered.

"Are you okay?" Alex asked.

No, I'm not okay, she wanted to scream. "No. No, I'm fine. Everything is—"

Thomas snatched the phone out of her hands.

Lily cried out, "No!"

But he was too quick for her. He ended the call and threw

her phone to the side. "Didn't you hear me say to end the call?"

Her hands were shaking. She looked down at the floor.

He didn't even let me say goodbye.

The phone started ringing.

Alex, calling back.

Thomas reached for the phone and shut it off.

Lily put her hands in the air. "I tried to end the conversation, but he kept talking . . ."

"You did not try!" He shouted and pounded his fist against the door.

Lily took a step back, bumping into the freezer behind her.

No one would come for her now.

Alex would do just as she asked, like always. If she didn't show up today, he wouldn't go after her—not because he didn't care—but because she had told him not to. There was nothing she wanted more than for him to ignore her words.

Her heart pounded like a racehorse as she tried to regain her composure. She put her chin in the air and took a step forward.

"Okay, I stuck to my end of the deal. Can I leave now? Alex won't contact me anymore. He'll do what I say."

"No, you're not leaving."

"But you said if I told him—"

"I know what I said, and I changed my mind."

"But *you* promised."

"I never promised anything. These are my terms, and I'm not letting you go yet."

"You can't keep me here. People will wonder where I am. They'll come for me."

"No one will come for you right now. Can't you see that?" He pointed to a folding chair in the corner. "Sit down."

Thomas still blocked the door, and the chances of escaping before he caught her were slim. Her phone was out of reach. Her ankle was still weak. There was no way she could overpower him. Her only option was to try to persuade him to let her go, even though he seemed more determined than ever to keep her here.

"Why are you doing this?"

"I want to talk about us."

Never, Lily wanted to choke out, but she held back and stared silently at Thomas's forehead, where perspiration was forming.

At that moment, the shop's landline began to ring. The phone was hanging in the back hallway where she had entered. A black rotary phone with a curly cord from years earlier that she hadn't bothered to take down. Though she rarely used it, she kept it for her older customers who sometimes still called in their orders.

Thomas turned around. "Who is calling?"

"Probably a customer. Or my mom." The phone kept ringing.

"Don't you have some kind of answering service?"

Lily shook her head. She hadn't set it up because it seemed pointless.

The phone continued ringing incessantly.

"Maybe I should answer," Lily said, trying to distract Thomas. "It must be a customer."

"Then answer it and hang up on them."

"If I hang up, they'll think there's something wrong."

"Then take the call and get rid of them."

Lily walked to the phone and picked it up. Her voice trembled as she tried to fake a cheerful greeting. "Hello, Lily's Chocolate Shop?"

"Lily." It was Alex. "Are you okay?"

She paused. He had remembered her landline. This was her one chance to alert him.

"No—no, I'm not . . . making any more chocolate-covered cherries this week. I'm so sorry. Maybe next time." Then she hung up.

She had no idea whether her words would be enough to alert Alex, but it was worth one last-ditch effort. She looked back at Thomas, her face masking her emotions. "Just a customer who had a question."

"Sit down again. We aren't done talking."

Lily didn't want to go back into the storage room. She stood frozen in the hallway. "We can talk out here, can't we?"

"No, we can't."

She refused. For once, she needed to stand up to him. She could no longer be a victim. She was willing to talk, but she was tired of him threatening, making her feel small and weak.

"Thomas, if you want to hold a civil conversation with me, then you need to stop ordering me around. You say you want to talk about us, but why would I even consider it when you're treating me like a child?"

"I'm upset because you won't listen to me." He grabbed her arm and pulled her toward the back room. Without warning, he yanked her arm harder, his fingertips biting into her flesh, pulling her away from freedom.

Suddenly, panic surged as her mind flashed back to the last time this had happened. As he forced her into the room, she tried to wrestle her arm from his grasp. "Thomas, please, stop pulling my arm. That hurts."

He didn't seem to hear her pleas. His grip burned into her flesh as he dragged her toward the chair. She decided, in that moment, to fight back, to try to escape. As she resisted, his strength overpowered her, catapulting her forward.

Her world tilted and shifted as she lost her balance and crashed against the chair. Her head was pounding, her eyes closed, when she heard a muffled sound from far away. A distant noise in the hallway, then the crash of a door opening.

Alex's voice called to her in the darkness. She wondered if the pounding in her head was causing her to imagine it. But when she looked toward the door, Alex had come for her.

Thomas turned around quickly, as Alex frantically looked from Thomas to her.

"What did you do to her?" Alex strode over to Thomas and grabbed him by his shirt.

"Nothing. She fell!" Thomas cowered under Alex's grip. "Tell him, Lily. Tell him how you fell down."

"Why don't I believe you?" Alex said. "I want you to stay away from Lily! Don't you ever touch her again." Alex shoved Thomas backward, causing him to stumble into the wall.

She hadn't ever seen Alex this angry.

He ran to Lily and knelt beside her. "Are you okay? Let me help you up."

As Alex lifted Lily, she saw Thomas escape out the door of the back room."

"Alex, he's leaving," Lily cried.

He stood, ready to chase him, but stopped and turned back to her. "I'm not leaving you alone. I'll call the police and let them deal with him. Besides, I don't want to do something I'll regret."

"I wish you would have. We both might feel better." When the sob broke from her body, she sank to the floor, where he wrapped his arms around her.

"Are you hurt? What did he do to you?"

"I'm not hurt, other than a bump to my head from when he shoved me into the chair and I fell."

"Oh, Lily, I'm so sorry. When you called and told me you never wanted to talk to me, something in your voice sounded off. Then I heard you cry no and the line went dead. I knew something was wrong."

"Why did you call back on the landline?"

"Your phone wasn't picking up, which isn't like you since you never turn off your phone. I jumped in the truck and headed this way. That's when I remembered your landline. When I asked if you were okay and you gave me that strange answer, that's when it hit me. He was the one who broke into your shop. I'd bet money on it."

"That's probably when he stole my spare key hidden in the

back room. He was waiting for an opportunity to talk to me alone. I had told everyone how the shop would be closed. He must have waited until I came in, then—" She choked on the last word, remembering the moment when she had realized she wasn't alone. This nightmare would haunt her for a long time.

Alex held her in his arms as she sobbed.

"I'm sorry," she said, between sobs. "I don't want to cry in front of you."

"Hey," he whispered, his face resting against her head. "You can always cry in front of me. You're safe now. We'll call the police and file a report, then get a restraining order."

She pulled away, suddenly aware how his closeness was making her feel. She had never felt this safe. "But what about today?"

"We can put off the final episode. It's okay. I don't want you to worry about anything else."

"No, I can do it. Just give me some time to catch my breath and go home."

"Are you sure? You don't have to do this, Lily." He let go of her to look into her eyes.

He was trying to give her space, honor her wishes, and make her feel safe. He would never betray her trust the way Thomas had.

Now, she wondered if she had lost him forever.

"I want to do this." If she was going to say goodbye to Alex, she wanted to at least follow through with her promise and see her new home. She rested her head against his chest, his arms wrapped around her. She wanted to be held like this forever.

CHAPTER TWENTY-EIGHT

LILY

When she showed up to film the final episode, nobody could tell what she had been through that day. She wasn't quite sure how it was possible, but she had managed to pull herself together, the least she could do for Alex and for herself.

To hide the surprise of her finished home, they had agreed to meet a few blocks from the house.

When Alex approached her on the sidewalk, his smile lit up, erasing every other thought from her mind.

She was dressed in a long white sundress, and her hair was loosely curled over her shoulders.

"You look amazing." He slid his hands in his pockets and looked her over. "On the Home Renovation Network, we say the house is the star of the show, but I'm pretty sure you'll be the star today."

He gave her hand a quick squeeze and left her to talk through details with the camera crew.

Her parents pulled up in their car with her siblings following. Her dad put down the car window and gave her a gentle smile. "You look nice, sweetie. I don't know how Alex could let you go after he sees you."

She held out her hand to her dad, and he gave it a gentle squeeze "Oh, Dad, Alex isn't letting me go. I'm the one who made the decision. It's best if we part ways after today."

Even when she said the words, something inside her throbbed, a painful reminder of everything she was losing. *Why was letting him go so hard when she knew it was for the best?*

"Mr. and Mrs. Woods, so glad you could be here today." Alex said, as he returned to Lily's side. "I think you're going to be just as surprised as Lily. You can meet us at the houses. I'll take Lily over."

Then he turned to her with his familiar smile that made her weak inside. "Ready to go?"

She looked into Alex's blue eyes and nodded. Even though he was the one in charge, his intensity softened to a tenderness in his gaze and a boyish, half-smile that reminded her of the guy she'd known in high school. She wanted to wrap her arms around him and hold on to this moment longer, but he stepped back and broke the spell.

"Would you like to walk with me?" He offered his arm to her. "This might be the last chance I'll get to talk to you before I leave tomorrow."

She hooked her arm through his. "You're leaving tomorrow? But I thought—" She stopped. It's not like she hadn't known this was coming. He had to leave.

I need to let him go.

"I didn't know you were leaving so soon."

"Time to move on to the next city," he said. "I don't have any reason to stay now that your home is complete."

But I want you to stay. She fought back the urge to tell him as they walked the tree-lined street toward her home in silence. She couldn't toy with his emotions or her own anymore—it wouldn't be fair. Clamping her mouth shut, she tried to enjoy this last walk with him, breathing their memory in deep, bottling it so she could save it forever.

When they approached her newly renovated home, a crowd was gathered on the street. They were smiling and laughing while her heart felt wrung out with the sadness of a chapter closed, an ending she did not want.

He turned to her, their last private moment together. "I hope you like your home as much as I liked fixing it up for you."

"I'm sure I will. But don't you have to blindfold me or something? I want the full reveal today."

He laughed. "Yes, the full reveal is yours." He pulled the blindfold from his pocket and wrapped it around her head, tying it gently.

"You're going to have to walk me to my parents. I can't see a thing."

He took her hand and gave it a gentle squeeze. "My pleasure."

As they drew closer, she could hear her sisters mingling with her parents and brother. Standing together, she suddenly realized what it was like to be surrounded by love. No matter what happened, she would still have her family, even if her heart had a huge hole when Alex left.

Alex cleared his throat and addressed the crowd that was buzzing with excitement. "Today we're here to do a double reveal of not one, but two homes. Are you ready for this?"

The crowd cheered as he went on. "Let's count down—three, two, one."

Everyone chanted with him as she slipped off the blindfold and opened her eyes to see her small fixer-upper transformed into an inviting home. She forgot all about the crowd and the cameras. She opened her mouth, speechless, and shook her head, captivated by the stunning cottage in front of her.

What used to be a crooked front stoop with peeling paint

was gone, replaced by a new front porch freshly painted and decorated with hanging baskets and window boxes overflowing with flowers.

"It's better than I imagined in my head." She walked toward the house, where Alex opened the front door. He had asked to take her in alone without anyone interrupting them.

"Oh, Alex," she gasped as she entered the cottage. Her home looked like it had dropped out of a magazine.

The hardwood floors gleamed with a smooth glow. Her walls were painted a light gray, decorated with open shelving and stacked with white dinnerware. The kitchen boasted new white cabinets and a marbled quartz countertop, just liked she had dreamed of. Everywhere she looked, there was something new; yet, Alex had worked hard to keep the charm that she loved in her old house.

When she turned back around to Alex, he was smiling at her. "Do you like it?"

"It's just incredible. You kept all my favorite parts of the house and made them even better."

That's when she noticed the stained glass window above the door, glowing where the sun caught the glass with brilliant colors.

"The window. It's . . . different." She slowly walked toward it, the colors dazzling in the light, reflecting reds and pinks across her white walls. "It's from Joshua's shop. The window I wanted. You made it work." She stood under it, finally seeing the picture for the first time. "I never noticed the details before. It's two doves flying together into the sunset. It's perfect, Alex. You did this for me?"

He was standing behind her, his hands in his pockets. "For you. With Joshua's encouragement. I know how you love old things."

She turned and took his hands. "This means the world to me."

"It's not over yet. Come outside. I have another surprise." He took her to the newly rebuilt deck facing the beach, where her parents and the rest of the crowd had gathered between the two houses. The new deck even had a wheelchair ramp so her dad could join them.

"I have one more surprise today," Alex announced to the crowd. "Originally, we were going to sell the house next door. But we've had a change of plans." He turned to Lily. "I know you wanted to make your home a safe place for your parents to visit. But then I thought, what if your parents didn't have to live across town? What if you could check on them anytime? We're giving them the house next door, so you can be close by all the time."

Lily's mouth fell open as she looked from Alex to her parents. "You're giving the house next door to Mom and Dad?"

Turning to her parents to wrap them in a hug, she couldn't hold back the tears that sprang to her eyes and fell down her face. Her mom joined her, wiping her mascara-smeared eyes, while her dad just beamed.

Becky put her hand on Alex's arm. "Much as we love our current home, we always dreamed of retiring on the beach. Thank you, Alex."

"You're welcome. It's the least I could do after all you've done. You were like a second family to me growing up. And now, my only family left in Wild Harbor."

Lily walked to Alex and wrapped her arms around him, her cheeks wet with tears. "I can't believe you're doing this. This is more than I could ever ask for."

He didn't say anything. He just held her tight. One last hug before he left for good. One treasured moment before he had to say goodbye.

CHAPTER TWENTY-NINE

ALEX

Alex sat on the deck of his rental condo for the last time, eating kung pao chicken out of a take-out box late at night while the waves gently lapped in the darkness. The big home reveal was done. The renovation schedule had been more demanding than any other home, but it had all been worth it to see the joy on her face.

But now it was time to head home. Even the mention of the word *home* seemed strange after spending so much time in Wild Harbor.

Funny how LA had never felt like it.

He needed to pack his suitcase, but had zero desire, like an invisible resistance was pinning him to his chair.

Tomorrow he would begin a new chapter, but somehow it didn't feel new. What did he have to look forward to?

Living out of a suitcase and eating takeout alone?

The thought made his stomach turn.

It's time to go, he prodded himself, but couldn't move. All he could think of was Lily.

He leaned forward and put his head in his hands, closing his eyes, trying to block her face from his mind. The more he tried to forget her, the more he thought about her. He was caught in a useless cycle of frustration.

He wondered if Lily was sitting in her newly remodeled home, looking at all the details he had so meticulously put in place for her. The stained glass window. The mirror in her bedroom. Or maybe, like him, she was looking at the beach, trying to accept the future.

When they had wrapped up today's episode, celebrating with a final party with the cast and crew, their goodbye had been rushed, words quickly spoken in a flurry of activity, while family and friends interrupted. There wasn't time for a stolen moment between him and her, where he could give her a real goodbye. In the end, all he had received was a quick hug and a thank you.

This wasn't how he wanted to leave. It crushed him to go.

How could their story end this way?

He heard the soft flutter of something nearby. The whisper of air, then stillness. A soft coo he could barely make out above the churn of the waves. He lifted his head from his hands, his eyes adjusting to the light of the full moon.

Two small figures had alighted on the edge of his deck. He could barely make out their shape, but their sound was distinct.

Mourning doves.

As a child, he had once found a nest in a woodpile and had been fascinated by how the mourning doves tended the nest together, taking turns, never leaving it alone. When he'd tried to approach, one dove had faked a broken wing as a distraction, then flew off when he came closer. He hadn't thought much about it at the time, but he was sure Joshua would have something to say.

Don't think it's just a coincidence. Nothing in life happens by accident.

Alex wanted to counter these arguments in his head, tired of Joshua' advice intruding into his thoughts. *Lots of things happen unexpectedly, Trina's accident. My father's death—*

The doves drew closer, almost within reach. But he held back, afraid of frightening the gentle birds away. They stood frozen, their beady eyes locked on his.

"What are you staring at?" he asked, annoyed that the birds seemed so interested.

Oh great, now I'm talking to birds.

The birds gave him one final look, then soundlessly rose together, swallowed by the black night, then rising into the moon's glow. A silhouette of two doves outlined by the gleaming moon, their figures distinct and familiar.

The window.

How could he be so blind?

It was there right in front of him. He tried to push it out of his head.

You told me to let go. I'm letting her go.

Then came the gentle reply: *Maybe you're letting go of the wrong thing.*

Even though it was late, he grabbed his keys and dashed out the door. No matter what happened, he'd try. He wanted to fight for her.

He'd been a fool to ever let her go.

WHEN HE PULLED up to Lily's home that night, the street outside was empty. The crowds that had gathered for the big day were long gone, leaving the charming beach cottage aglow with a solitary light.

Walking onto her porch and quietly knocking, he saw her through the window, the golden light illuminating her against the darkness.

When the door opened, she froze for a second. "Alex? What are you doing here? I thought—"

"I was leaving?" he asked.

"Yes."

He slipped his hands in his pockets. "I didn't feel right about how I left things with you today."

"Me too."

"It seemed—"

"Rushed?" she asked.

He smiled, realizing they were completing each other's sentences.

They had always had an uncanny sense of what the other person was about to say.

Lily tucked her hair behind her ear. "I'm sorry there wasn't more time, especially after all you did for me."

"Lily, I'm not here to say goodbye . . . because I'm not leaving." He looked at her, the moonlight highlighting her face, the murmur of waves in the distance.

Her face held an expression he couldn't read in the darkness, but her eyes flashed with emotion, like she was pushing back the current. "What? But your flight—it's *tomorrow*. You have a house to renovate in Seattle."

He put his hands on her shoulders. "Do you know how I feel every time I look at you? Do you know all I can think about is how it feels to hold you in my arms? I've been trying to convince myself that leaving you is the right thing to do. But I'm tired of doing the *right* thing. I love you. I love all of you. And I'm not leaving this time."

"But you can't stay—"

"Do you see this window?" He pointed to the stained glass treasure from Joshua's shop. "It's here because a man loved a woman, and then when he thought all was lost, he found love again."

"But they're not us."

"I'm not just talking about them. We have our own story." He cupped her face in his hands. "I just need to know if you want this as much as I do."

She whispered, "I want to say it, but I don't know—"

He put his fingers on her lips. "You don't need to know how. We'll figure it out together. Just tell me you want me to stay."

She looked into his eyes. "Yes, please stay."

Then he leaned down and gently kissed her lips. Once. Twice. Then longer, until they were melting into each other, his hands slipping down her neck and onto her back, into an embrace that was overwhelming him.

She pulled away suddenly, her brows furrowed. "But what will you tell your crew and agent? They're counting on you."

"I'll tell them the truth. That I fell in love with you."

"They'll resent me, Alex."

"No, they won't. Because I'm making sure the show—and their jobs—will go on without me. I decided that there was one person who would want my job more than I do and who's totally qualified to lead the show. That's Alli. She's always wanted to be the host, honestly. This news will make her day. I'll be the happiest man alive because I'll have you."

He leaned down and gave her a tender kiss again, her lips warm against his, like a sweet taste he could never tire of.

In the distance, above the sound of the rolling waves, he thought he heard the gentle sound of doves. It drifted away as quickly as birds flying off into the night, leaving him with the slow, steady beat of love, and the realization that all he longed for was right here after all.

CHAPTER THIRTY

LILY

W hen Lily woke the next day, she lay in bed, enjoying the sunlight spilling across the covers in a golden glow. Last night seemed like a dream.

Did Alex promise to stay in Wild Harbor? Was he really giving up everything for her?

She sat up in bed and grabbed her phone. A message from Alex was waiting.

Alex: Good morning, beautiful. I've invited your whole family over to enjoy coffee and muffins at nine. I hope you don't mind. Wanted to break the news to them. Can't wait to see you then.

Lily checked her watch. Eight thirty. *Overslept, again.*

This time, Lily didn't care. Last night was worth it.

She slipped on a pretty floral dress with some sandals. Putting on the last touch of lip gloss, she heard a knock at her door and opened it.

Alex stood on the other side, holding a box of muffins and a coffee. "I bring this as a peace offering." He handed her the beverage. "I hope you're not mad at me."

"Mad at you? Why would I be?"

"I didn't ask you to host your family for breakfast. But I knew if we were going to tell them, we couldn't wait."

"No, I love this idea. And knowing how nosy my sisters are, the news can't wait."

They walked to the back deck facing the lake, where Alex put the muffins down on the patio table. He crossed to Lily. "I didn't give you a proper greeting."

"Only a greeting?"

He grabbed her by the waist. "You get a special one."

As he wrapped his arms around her, she leaned into him, feeling the calming presence of his embrace as he kissed her lips. *Oh, how she loved this.*

A knock broke up their tender moment. She looked up at him, frowning. "Already? I was just getting comfortable."

"There will be plenty more of this." He gave her another quick kiss. "Especially since I'm not leaving town."

She moved to the door and opened it. Cassidy was dressed in a loose bohemian blouse with a pair of shorts, while Megan was ready for another day at the office, attired in black dress pants and a crisp white shirt. Her sisters couldn't be any more different in their personalities and their style.

"This better be big news, sis." Megan followed Lily. "I was writing a story until two in the morning, and now I need to do interviews for another article. The life of a writer is *not* glamorous." She looked around. "Where's the coffee? I need some —bad."

Lily linked her arm through Megan's and led her toward the deck. "Coffee is on the patio table. So, last night's home reveal didn't make the paper, huh?"

"Quite the opposite." Megan smiled. "I was writing *your* story last night. You'll read it on the front page later today."

Cassidy grabbed Lily's arm. "What's the big news? I thought last night couldn't be topped."

Lily stopped them before they opened the door to the deck. "Well, it's probably not as big as finding out Mom and Dad are moving in next door. But I wanted to make sure you were the first to know."

Cassidy spotted Alex waiting on the deck. "Wait a minute." Her eyes widened. "This isn't about Alex, is it?"

"I'm not telling until everyone arrives." Lily gave her sisters a secretive smile as their mouths dropped open.

"That's not the way this works." Megan held up her first finger. "Number one: We are *your* sisters. Number two: No secrets between us. Wasn't that the pact we made in elementary school?"

Lily laughed. "It was. But how about coffee first? Alex brought muffins to help me stall."

"This is totally not fair!" Megan threw up her arms as she made a beeline for the caffeine.

As they joined Alex outside, Becky, Bill, and Matt arrived and gathered around the patio table. The morning sun and hot coffee warmed them as they watched the locals walk the beach.

"What's the reason you called us here this morning?" Matt sipped his coffee. "Last night's surprise wasn't enough?"

Lily set down her cup and folded her hands, her heart thundering in her chest. "So we wanted to tell you the news. Alex has decided to stay in Wild Harbor because . . ."

She looked around at their expectant faces and suddenly felt overwhelmed with gratitude for her family. Through all their difficulties, she still had the people she loved most around her, and now, that would be completed with Alex.

"Because . . ." Alex cut in, locking eyes with her. "Because I'm in love with Lily and want to be with her."

Lily looked at him, surprised.

"I'm sorry." Alex smiled, reaching for her hand. "Should I not have said that yet?"

"No," Lily said, a grin spreading across her face. "I am so glad you did." She cupped his face in her hands and kissed him. She didn't care who saw them anymore.

"Well, it's about time," Megan blurted out.

"I knew it!" Matt exclaimed, standing. "Didn't I tell you guys they were going to end up together?"

"Oh, how beautiful." Cassidy raised her hands to her lips to hold back the tears.

Her parents were beaming, not saying anything.

Lily stepped away from Alex and turned to her dad and mom. Reaching across the table, she grabbed her father's hand. "You and Mom are both very quiet about the news. I hope you're not disappointed."

"Disappointed?" Her mom slapped the table. "Oh, no, honey. We always knew Alex was a keeper. We just wondered when *you* would figure it out."

Lily looked at her father. "Dad, you're not saying anything."

"I-I'm speechless." Her dad chuckled, his eyes gleaming with joy. He had regained some of his clarity in the moment as he gazed at his daughter. "There are no words when you see your children happy."

She wrapped her arms around her dad in a bear hug. During the last year, they had been through so much together. His stroke. Her shop. A broken heart and the fixer-upper they had dreamed of restoring together.

Her mom leaned toward Alex, a sparkle in her eyes. "Not to pry, but when's the wedding?"

"Mom!" Lily shook her head. "How embarrassing. We're just dating."

Becky gave Alex a quick wink. "All I'm saying is don't wait forever if you know she's the one."

"Don't worry," Alex laughed as he wrapped his arm around Lily's waist. "I'm the last person who will want to wait."

"So, what's going to happen to the show?" Matt grabbed another muffin. "And your TV career?"

"I'm leaving the show, and Alli will be taking over as *The Property Bachelorette*. She's always wanted to be the host. When I called her this morning, I told her, 'I've decided to step down from the show, but before you say anything, I talked to the producers and recommended they offer you the job as host. The good news is . . . they agreed.'

"All I could hear was silence on the other end, so I asked, 'Alli, are you okay with that?' She said, 'I can't believe you'd do that for me.' Of course, what I didn't tell her is that I'm starting my own show, because this isn't the end of my TV career. I hope to flip beach homes in the area. The network is interested in talking more about it, so we'll see what happens. For now, I'm perfectly content pursuing my TV career in Wild Harbor."

"Perfect," Matt replied. "You can join our guys' group that meets at the coffee shop."

"Are you sure they'll want to take me if I'm not single?"

"Positive. Maybe you can help the rest of us with our love lives. Be our relationship guru."

"Considering I almost ruined the best thing that ever happened to me, you might not want my advice," Alex said with a smirk.

"We need a picture together to remember this day." Becky pulled out her phone. "Everyone, gather around your dad."

"Why don't I take the picture, Becky?" Alex reached out his hand. "Then you can be in it."

"No, Alex. I want you in the picture with Lily."

"But I'm not part of the family—"

"You are now. And one of the first rules is you don't argue with Mom."

Lily stifled a giggle as Alex joined the family, huddled around Dad's wheelchair.

"Welcome to the Woods family." Matt gave Alex a slap on the back.

Lily locked her hand with Alex's and gave it a squeeze.

This was everything he had ever wanted.

EPILOGUE

ALEX

2 MONTHS LATER

When Alex arrived at Lily's house, he took a deep breath to steady his nerves.

Not that he had any doubts now.

He just wanted things to be perfect.

He walked through the white gate on his way to the beach and was reminded of the first time he had ventured through it with Lily, the night they'd had their first date.

Although Lily wasn't home from work yet, he settled on the same spot where they had enjoyed a picnic overlooking the lake. As he spread the beach blanket on the white sand, he rehearsed the words he had planned all week.

"These last few months have been magical—"

No, wait. That sounds too cheesy.

Why was it so hard to say what he really felt?

If he didn't muster the courage to ask today, he wouldn't be able to wait any longer. It would drive him crazy to carry around this ring another day.

Suddenly, two hands covered his eyes, as a familiar voice behind him said, "Please don't think I'm a strange woman trying to sneak up on you. But I couldn't resist surprising you." Lily released her hands and sat down in the sand next to him.

"You're early." He wrapped his arms around her and gave her a kiss.

"I almost jumped out to startle you, but I thought I'd be nice."

"You're lucky I didn't pull out some wrestling moves and flip you over my shoulder." He grinned.

"Hmm. I might not have minded." She shoved him, laughing. "As long as you're gentle, of course."

"I'm not sure that's the point of wrestling." He grabbed her hands. "The goal is to overcome your opponent. You know, pin them down."

"That's what I'm trying to do. Maybe I need to freshen up my wrestling moves," she teased.

"No need. You already have," he said, suddenly more serious.

She looked at him with those blue eyes that always did a number on his heart. "So, what's the special occasion?"

"I wanted to remember the first time we enjoyed a date here. If I get this right, it will be the only thing that matters."

She narrowed her gaze.

He reached in his pocket and pulled out the box. "I know how much you like things that are old. Vintage, as you like to say. Things that you see potential in when most people don't. Joshua taught me that beauty can be found in brokenness. That restoration is possible after something has been marred beyond belief. Both of us have endured struggles, and we've built walls to protect us from facing hurt again. But I'm seeing how much your love is changing me. Breaking down my walls. Making me a better man. I want us to be together forever."

He opened the box and showed her the ring.

She caught her breath. "It's beautiful, Alex. Where did you get this? It's not like anything I've seen before."

"Joshua's had it in his shop forever. He said it was waiting for the right couple. He found the ring years ago, slightly bent, but the diamond was in perfect shape. Whatever happened to the ring to bend it out of shape didn't affect the stone, because diamonds are made to endure almost anything. He said it would take a strong couple, who had been through adversity, to understand its value.

"When I heard that, I knew it was the right one. Now I'm just dying to hear an answer."

"I'm waiting for you to ask," she said, her smile lighting up her eyes. "Because you haven't popped the question yet."

"What? I guess I'm so nervous, I completely forgot." He got down on one knee. "Lily Woods, would you marry me? Because you'd make me the happiest man alive if you agreed."

Lily searched his face as tears began to stream down her cheeks. "Yes, a thousand times over, yes."

She moved onto her knees and wrapped her arms around his neck, kissing him hard, falling into him, filling his whole being with joy.

She pulled away from his embrace and gently stroked his cheek. "I never dreamed I could be this happy. That my heart could feel this secure. That I would feel this loved. This held."

He kissed her again, harder this time, until she gently pulled away.

"When are we going to tell everyone? You know Megan will want the scoop for the paper first. Then the press will pick it up. But I want Mom and Dad to know first."

"Your parents already know. When I asked your dad for permission, he decided to make me sweat and hesitated before answering. Then he gave me a slap on the back and laughed, saying, of course, I could marry you, he just wanted to see what

I would do under pressure. For a few seconds, I thought he was going to say no."

"Sounds like Dad."

"I've already told your family to meet us at the chocolate shop, along with a few friends. I told them get ready to celebrate."

"What?" Lily sprang up off the ground. "Let's go. I can't wait to show them my ring and start planning our wedding. I can't even believe I'm saying that. *Our* wedding. I never thought it would happen."

She grabbed his hand and pulled him toward her car. "Come on."

"I'm all yours, but we can't leave our stuff here."

"Oh, right." She folded the blanket quickly. "I feel like this is our spot now. The place we'll return to with our children, maybe even our grandchildren."

She stopped and put her hand on his cheek, moving closer to him. "I love you, Alex," she said, her tone suddenly tender. "More than anything."

"More than chocolate?" A smile played on the corners of his lips.

She smiled. "Yes, even more than chocolate."

She leaned in and gave him a tender kiss, one that was different from before. It wasn't urgent or demanding, but instead offered something more. A token of her love, a promise of forever.

Read on for a sneak peek of **Summer Nights in Wild Harbor** and find out what happens in book two when Lily's sister, Megan, falls in love. Get the book on Amazon.

Escape to the small town of Wild Harbor in this summer beach romance about Megan and Finn finding their happily ever after in book two.

Did you love Lily and Alex's story?
Leave a review on Amazon!

Get hot book deals and a free story by joining Grace Worthington's clean romance newsletter at graceworthington.com.

SNEAK PEEK OF SUMMER NIGHTS IN WILD HARBOR

Megan Woods knows that fairy tales don't come true.

So, when a handsome stranger shows up to rescue her from a blind date gone wrong, she figures there has to be a catch. Turns out, he's her newest competition at the newspaper. Before the annoyingly charming Finn Avery ruined her prospect for a promotion, Megan believed she had the editor-in-chief position in the bag. As far as she's concerned, their relationship is strictly business. But Finn's not anything like she expected. He's making her forget why falling in love would be a bad idea.

Finn Avery is looking for a fresh start. He moved to Wild Harbor looking to escape from his past, only to find out he's been paired with spitfire Megan Woods. Finn needs to prove himself as a reporter, and that means winning over his gorgeous coworker, even though she seems immune to his charms. Their connection is immediate, but his past holds secrets that have taught him not to take a chance on love.

Opposites in every way, romance is the last thing on both their minds. But when they're forced to team up for Wild Harbor's biggest summer event, the sparks fly.

Can Finn let go of his past in order to risk his heart again? Can Megan find her happily ever after in the arms of her fiercest opponent? Can this headstrong pair reconcile their differences and write their own happily ever after—on and off the page?

Buy the book so you don't miss book two in the Wild Harbor Beach Series: *Summer Nights in Wild Harbor,* now on Amazon.

A NOTE FROM GRACE

A story is a magical thing—it offers an escape from your worries, it tugs on your emotions, it lifts you away, like an enchanted carpet. I wanted to write this series after vacationing on Lake Michigan. I fell in love with its small towns and white sand beaches. The quaint beach homes and the families who had been there for generations showed me there was something special woven into the fabric of their lives. I wanted to capture that kind of community in the Wild Harbor Beach Series.

But even more, I wanted you to escape into a story about the power of love. How it heals us. Transforms us. Restores us.

I believe that kind of love still exists.

—Grace

ACKNOWLEDGMENTS

Thank you to…

My family. My life with you is richer. Thank you for coming along with me on this crazy writing journey. You show me that creativity and story matter, especially when it has a redemptive ending and points to the source of love.

My mom. I'm grateful that you shared your love of reading with me. Thanks for taking me to the library as a girl, so I could learn to love books.

My wise editor, Kim Peterson, and my supportive beta readers, Joy Martz, Heidi Lanter, Michelle McCubbins, Thelma Nienhuis, Denise Long. Your immensely helpful feedback has made this book better. Thank you to Emily Poole for giving this story a final proofread.

Kristen Ingebretson for the beautiful cover design. Your work is always stunning.

My readers who are willing to pick up this book and give a new series some love. You don't know how grateful I am to have your support. Without you, there would be no Wild Harbor Beach Series. Your support means the world.

ABOUT THE AUTHOR

Grace Worthington writes sweet love stories by the fireplace in her ninety-year-old brick home. She has a degree in English and theatre and dreams of the beach and good books, especially if they're together. She resides with her husband, two children, and an overly friendly goldendoodle in Indiana. For free books, go to graceworthington.com

Did you get your FREE story from the Wild Harbor Beach Series? Join Grace's list and snag this free sweet romance story. Go to graceworthington.com.

Made in the USA
Columbia, SC
16 October 2021

47297324R00138